Guardian
Unmasked

T.D. Raufson

Printed in the United States of America
First Printing, 2020
ISBN: 978-1-7327863-3-2

Published by Twin Cedars Enterprises, LLC.

DEDICATION

To every fantasy book lover ever.

CONTENTS

ACKNOWLEDGMENTS

Writing is an ever challenging but rewarding exercise. I tell people that I write so that I can keep the voices in my head quiet. I always enjoy writing although it is not always fun. Sometimes I chase my characters around trying to figure out where they want to go. Other times I am in synch with them, and the pages flow easily. Because of this form of insanity, I thank those in my family who know the symptoms and how to deal with them. Primarily I thank them for knowing how to deal with their own reactions to them as there is no cure for me.

I want to thank my editor, Ruth Jackson for keeping me aware of both the right and wrong words that must be part of my writing. It has been a good year creating this world and the characters that populate it. I appreciate her coming along for the adventure.

I cannot acknowledge enough the support of my wife. Susan, thank you for sharing the sometimes unending conversations about characters, plots, ideas, irritations, and everything else that comes with being married to a writer. I know you understand because we are both married to writers, but I still must tell you that I appreciate you and all that you do.

The list of others who have somehow contributed to my ability to create these stories is far too long to present here. I will simply say thank you to all of you as a final acknowledgement.

GUARDIAN'S ESCAPE

Caravan towns reeked. They smelled of everything you didn't want touching you, and Roark hated entering them. The smells of the woods and glens were more pleasing. In a slight movement the fighter shifted the short sword on the belt and the bow beneath the pack. With a shuffle of muscular hips, tired from the walk out of the pass, the belt settled into a less irritated spot. The sculpted leather armor covered the guardian's chest and highlighted muscles even though it covered an equally well-fitting padded gambeson. The selection of daggers and blackjacks, hanging on the belt, warned anyone that might want to mess with the train to move along.

As much as caravan towns were distasteful, they always meant payday. Part of earning that pay was knowing how to enter a town so that everyone understood to leave this train alone.

Roark looked back at the bedraggled chain of wagons and the herd of people who followed. They spread out along the trace for nearly a quarter mile.

Every few hundred feet along the train walked a trusted member of the caravan's guard. Sworn to protect the people and cargo, they were all bound by blood to get the train through the passes without unacceptable loss. But, more than that, they had all sworn their lives in a far more binding ceremony to Roark. Each one of them owed the slender mercenary a life debt, and some several times over.

With a motion of the fingers on a raised hand, Malich, the first man in the protective line and second in command, passed a message to those guardians.

The signal elicited immediate reaction down the line. Arrows slipped silently from quivers and onto bow strings. Swords were drawn by the guards closer to the train. Between the two extremes, poleaxes came up to form a protective barrier. Each man became an example of the death that awaited anyone who approached the travelers.

Boys— gathered along the edge of the roads leading to the terminus of the Path of Mists—pointed and whispered as the men established their traditional show of force with flourish and style. In a few more yards the protectors would hand their charge over to the real thieves, the men who would value the trainload of miscellaneous goods the hopeful travelers brought with them. Over half of the train were hopefuls. Roark's team was directly responsible for the rest by contract signed and paid at the other end.

In support of the whole train, Roark drew a bow, nocked an arrow to the sinew string, but waited to draw it. No need to wear down muscles until a threat appeared. They never really expected a threat in the towns. There were far better places on the pass to take a caravan that held no risk other than the Guardians, but the show was important for morale and recruiting. It also made it easier to charge those waiting for escort services the asking price. As the other soldiers played to the crowd, Roark scanned the covered entrance to the caravanserai's office to see what was awaiting them there. The standard rabble were lined up to organize their own trip through the mountains, and the soldier groaned internally. They never got a break. There was always another collection of humanity that wanted to move across those mountains thinking making it to another town might mean a better life or even passage out. Roark knew, from observation, that no one who needed to could ever afford to really leave the mountains. The fare was higher in the border towns. The pay was the same, and the rabble roamed the borders sweeping up stragglers who tried to break through the net in the hand full of openings. So, on the fringe, it was even harder to get out.

As a Guardian, the risk might become a faster path to a better life, but it appeared to be no closer and there was no end to the repetitive cycle of escort jobs waiting, not when you were good at it. Now, at seventeen, the sudden realization of hopelessness unearthed memories of a dream of more than constant vigilance. A warrior could only take so much interaction with thieves and brigands who preyed on the weak and undefended. There had been the fleeting idea, early on, of becoming the hero who actually saved some rich prince or even a distant ruler. In payment, Roark would earn freedom.

The sad truth was that caravans were mostly filled with the dregs of humanity, not royalty waiting to pass out wards. There had been many caravan whores and easy men who sought their own breed of saving among the Guardians. Some had found what they sought, but none represented any real hope of escape from the cycle of the passes.

The point of the nocked arrow drew a line along the next ragged queue of waiting travelers. It measured the value and risk of each one until it stopped. A cold chill rushed up Roark's back. The riskiest cargo that had ever pulled into a caravan town was surrounded by hopeful waifs looking for a taste of patronage. Ten men dressed in immaculate field plate and scarlet scarves stood on either side of a glistening wooden carriage covered in gold and silver gilt. A thief worth his tools could shave enough gold off the sides of the royal wagon to live a comfortable life away from the mountains and the passes. The ten guards stood with halberds scraping the sky and swords nearly dragging the ground. Sadly, Roark knew, they would never make it along the rough trails ahead of them. Experience said, rogue archers would take them out before they could draw a sword. Then, their brothers-in-arms would slither down their ropes and cull the carriage and its valuable flesh cargo from the train. They wouldn't have to touch any of the other wagons, and there would be no way for the caravan Guardians to protect it. It was a gleaming omen of failure that no real leader would allow in a train, no matter the offered reward. Not even if its very presence promised life out of the mountains.

The wind turned cold as the experienced warrior realized the caravan agent was holding the signed papers. He should know better. Roark looked back at Malich and motioned at the glittering wagon. Without any hesitation Malich shook his head and mimed the look like a man who had taken too much sweet root along the trail, but then his face changed. The skilled chief-of-staff's face turned pale as if his dead mother had walked across the opening. Roark looked back towards the line of new travelers.

A door along the side of the wagon's polished wall was open. A delicate hand pointed out at the arriving crowd. The slender fingers glistened white in the sunlight without any help from jewelry. Roark had never seen such a clean hand. A white sleeve adorned with embroidered blue and golden lace descended from the wrist to the bottom of the door. A soft, young arm extended from the angelic hand back into the sleeve, charging Roark's imagination of what delicate flesh rested just beyond that sleeve's terminus. The door opened with a freshening breeze that exposed an amazing and terrifying view of the angel's booted foot and a pink white calf. Roark stared a moment, stunned that the carriage that was already a threat to everyone's safety could be any worse, but there was no doubt that in that perilous moment it was. The delicate female cargo in that doomed wagon was not even safe in this town.

The arrowhead tracked up from the view that could cost a man his life. The only man who had observed it was Malich, and he was actively rallying the men into a circular defensive wall with hand signs. Whomever had risked this woman's life so deserved to have his skin flayed from his back with a rusty file. No one so delicate as this survived the passes, and any who tried to protect her was equally cursed. Why had anyone allowed such a flower into this brutal arena?

"Gaylan!" Roark's shout echoed like a curse. "Close that up if you value your skin."

The agent standing next to the elegant and priceless hand jumped at the command as if he had been struck. He seemed to shiver at the threat and glared back at Roark.

The caravan leader drew the bow back to the ear and aimed the bodkin point just below the agent's unarmored shoulder blade. Roark knew the result of the shot from this close. The arrow would pierce him and nail him to the wood panel of the royal coach independent of a rib that might happen to get in the way. The agent's face turned white. He knew the same thing. The hand retreated into the darkness of the coach as the agent turned to speak up into the darkness, finally blocking the enticing view that had driven Roark to anger. In a moment the door was closed and the agent was walking toward the wall of protective men.

"You forget your place Roark. I'm the agent. You are just the guide."

"I'll guide your soul to the devil and his minions if you risk that woman and my men again."

"She's safe with her guards, you paranoid dolt."

"She has not been safe since that ridiculous invitation to rape pulled into this town and you know it. My paranoia pays your ridiculous rates. You show that woman's calf to the world again, and she will never leave this town alive. She may not now. Don't you feel the threat?"

"You can't be serious. There's no threat here. Not in town."

As if the man's words were a cue, an arrow thudded into the chest of the guard standing just ahead of the carriage door. Another pinned the driver of the coach to his seat and guaranteed the coach would not move from its place in the train. Of course the brigands would attack the coach and ignore the guards approaching. As Roark had predicted, only the guards protecting the coach were falling in series around their charge.

"What other idiot mistakes have you made, Gaylan," Roark asked, spinning around to aim the bow in the most obvious direction of the attackers.

Roark's trained eye caught movement in the trees just as another arrow thudded into the polished wood behind the door panel. With micro adjustments to the string, an inhale, and then a controlled release, the arrow leaped from the bow. It was away and another arrow was in the riser in a quick breath. The first arrow intercepted the running attacker just below his ear, stopping his run from the forest and changing it into a flopping fall to the dirt. In another breath the attackers would turn from the falling guards around the coach and start attacking the Guardians who were approaching. There was little time remaining to act.

Roark covered the rest of the distance to the coach in a burst of priceless energy, keeping the bow pointed toward the enemy. Malich stepped in without a pause, and the men started mowing down attackers like the grim reaper's merciless scythe.

The next arrow twanged away from Roark's bow on the run and nailed an approaching attacker to a tree. The gurgling scream and froth of blood that exploded from the young man's mouth verified that there was no need for another arrow.

In two long steps, the running warrior was up onto the driver's seat.

A hard stomp to the shaft released the trapped driver.

The freed body slipped down the opposite side of the carriage, releasing the coach to be guided from the encroaching horde. With a whistle and a tug on the secured reins, Roark had the frightened horses moving. They did not need much encouragement to move and the jerk of forward motion nearly unsettled the new driver. Roark braced and rode the bucking coach as it jerked out of the train over the bodies of its guards. With another whistle the horses jerked forward in an agonizingly slow acceleration toward the entrance to the high northern pass. Roark was executing a long-planned emergency escape route and hoped Malich would recognize it. There was no time to send a signal, but Roark was confident his First would immediately know. The plan would get the coach to a place where they could defend it better than the middle of the smelly town and remove the prize from around the arriving train that was now threatened more than it ever had been. They still had to get paid.

An arrow nicked the wool tunic. It glanced off the armor beneath, but the force tugged at the soldier's delicately balanced body and almost ended the escape. It did succeed in slowing the horses, but quick attention saved them from completely stopping. The horses nickered in irritation at the confusing orders, but only momentarily slowed before continuing the accelerating race to the north.

Trees enclosed the trail as the horses challenged the still standing rider. Screams from the enclosed coach verified the passengers were not happy, but they were alive. They were now mostly safe from arrows that would more likely hit a tree limb than the departing driver. Roark took a precious moment of concentration on the trail to identify who had organized the attack. The style of shaft work verified that the attackers were not from the ranges that housed the Pass of Mists. They would not know about the watering stage at the top of the ridge. Even if they tracked the distinct trail the coach left, Roark would turn it into an advantage.

As the forest swallowed the coach deeper into its protection, Roark looked back to verify they were now alone. The four horses had given them the lead they needed. With a relaxation of the reins, the beasts' run turned into a more controlled canter and the warrior finally settled into the blood-soaked seat. This coach would not be able to navigate the roads of the Northern Pass. That meant they would have to abandon it, and Roark suddenly had the start of a plan if the occupants would cooperate.

~~~

The coach came to a stop. Footsteps on the driver's bench told Elsa that he was getting down and her opportunity was approaching. She looked out the open window in the door and quickly completed her preparations. She wrapped her robe around her bare shoulders and took a deep breath. With a nod to the two women on the other side of the coach she opened the door and stepped out into the shaded sunlight. Dappled spots of light penetrated a heavy cover of green that was far over her head, creating a very different environment compared to the town they had stopped in to arrange the caravan over the Spine.

She stepped gingerly onto the sand, dirt, and leaves of a clearing. With a nervous inhale she realized how far away from the town they really were. The first thing that struck her was the improvement in the smell. The second was the cooling breeze that rushed up under her robe and encouraged a running chill and goose flesh to break out all over her naked body. She pulled her robe closer to her and looked at the cause of the chill, wishing a little more sun would break through the canopy above her. An enormous waterfall cascaded down the mountain that rose up to the right and away from the road, breaking over hundreds of outcroppings and thrusting spurs of rock that created a myriad of smaller falls and a wide spray of water that ultimately roared into the broad pool where the coach was now parked. The road turned west here and crossed the stream running from the fall fed pool. A wooden bridge that Elsa doubted would hold their carriage crossed the stream before it fell again into the deeper valley beyond the road. If the situation had not become so dire, the location would have been a beautiful place to stop and rest. She would enjoy a break with fresh bread and cheese here. Elsa forced herself to ignore the distracting landscape and focus on the situation. Bread, cheese, and wine were not what had her standing in the clearing in only her robe.

The brigand captor who had taken them on the racing getaway was drawing water from the pool in two fabric buckets that hung on a pole next to the water for just that reason.

His long black hair escaped beneath a metal, fur-lined cap, but was reined in by a thong of leather. It fell down his slight but tall back in a single shock that stopped at his waist. The woolen tunic bagged around his chest and jumbled into a roll over the belt. Numerous daggers, knives, and other tools of the brigand's trade filled the belt and seemed to warn that this man knew all of those varied skills.

A short sword hung on the left side in a leather frog that allowed him to draw it quickly but also wear it nearly straight down his leg. Leather britches and high boots completed the outfit. The tight fit of both drew her attention. The shapely legs hidden under the baggy woolen tunic promised this brigand might be quite an impressive— if small— specimen, but none of that changed her first opinion. The killer with the buckets was a young boy, probably seventeen years old, who was obviously dangerous and well-armed.

He turned from the water with the filled buckets and walked back toward the horses. A shadow of stubble ran from his ears across his chin and indicated that he shaved occasionally when able and chose not to wear a full beard. It was a choice that puzzled her. His bald face would cause him trouble in many areas around the realm and assuredly in the castle they had left a week before. A beard was a masculine trademark, and she knew few men who chose not to let the horrible nests grow until they hid most of their face.

For the obvious years that this man had been a Guardian, there was an amazing absence of scars on his face. That alone revealed a prowess with the weapons arrayed at his waist. His eyes made her heart jump in her chest. She had expected the angry and often dull-witted eyes afforded most warriors who could not trouble through the mental challenge of untying a corset. But these eyes, caught in a moment of thought as he worked, were anything but dull. A shiver of fear raced up her spine to slam into her fluttering heart. As an afterthought she noted that those troubling eyes were an emerald she had not often seen amongst men, and they actually seemed capable of more expression even than the face which was expressively working on some problem beyond the horses and their care. Behind the sparkling green though, Elsa could see the hidden coldness of reality. This young man had seen death, certainly the kind caused by others, likely the kind delivered by his own hand.

Elsa prided herself on reading men and knowing what they wanted. The depth of this one's eyes made her pause. They had assumed the driver who had taken them was a dull, stupid brute; completely harmless when faced with female charm and guile. She was hardly ever wrong, but in this case she had to be. What brigand ever paused to tend the horses when such a prize awaited him?

He looked around at his surroundings and stopped next to the lead horse when he saw her standing beside the carriage.

"So, brigand, what are your intentions?"

Elsa allowed the front of the robe to slide away from her neck and expose just the top of the cleft of her cleavage. The villain's eyes did not follow her action. The galloping shiver raced up her spine again. His ever cautious and thoughtful eyes darted around the carriage as if she might be in danger. Confusion joined the fear in her head.

"I'm no brigand, Lady. I'm the Guardian you and your charge were hiring back in town." The alto tones of the voice surprised her further. This boy would struggle among the baritone and be-whiskered men of her land. "A band of brigands attacked the staging area, and I've secured your safety."

"Any man could say the same out here with no proof. How do I know you tell the truth?"

She allowed the breeze to tug the robe away from her leg, exposing her naked calf up to her knee. She knew that would attract the eye of any man alive. This one's casual glance angered her as much as it scared her. What would draw his attention to her fully if not that? Would she have to drop her entire robe to draw him in, or was he just there to kill them? Did he care nothing for the pleasures even the most ruthless men would never ignore? She knew death would come only after brigands such as he had exhausted their passions. She shivered at that horrifying thought. For her trap to work he had to be drawn in, and so far he had not even set down his buckets.

"You're alive and not raped. Is that not proof enough of what I say?"

She felt her face shade at his unguarded words, but confusion and fear didn't allow her to believe him. This was a trick. She allowed the robe to open more, showing her deep cleft, but she stopped short of giving away the prize too soon. She wanted him interested, not out of control. This very act had saved their lives two villages before, and she had only had to go this far.

"You're a crude beast." Her words were accusatory, but her tone was inviting as if to indicate she found his brutishness arousing. The truth was not far off. She was excited by his very indifference. She had never met a man with such control. She was starting to feel a little insulted.

He had to commit to the act, or they were in serious trouble, and they would never get back to the safety of the palace guard and the rest of the caravan. She dropped her robe on the left side a little farther giving the first glimpse of the prize. The crest of her pink aureole just broke over the blue fabric, and she allowed the front to open above her knee which was an unheard of exposure in her home. If the palace guard had seen it, she would be branded a harlot and cast out into the filthy streets. The risks she took for her Lady were getting far too dangerous.

Her pulse quickened as she realized this desperate act had drawn the killer's attention. His eyes quickly took in the exposed leg that darted back under the robe. With that view gone, his eyes settled on her partially exposed chest. Her shoulder was now completely uncovered. She may as well have been lying back in a whore's crib awaiting her next customer.

He set down the buckets in a rush that startled her as he closed the distance between them. A warmth rushed through her loins, and she felt awkward that she might actually be considering this beast an able and interesting partner. Her flush was matched by the approaching man. His mouth opened slightly. She had his attention now, keeping it would not be a problem. She could not speak for her virtue.

With her eyes she motioned him forward, but he stopped.

"You're playing a dangerous game. A brigand would have already claimed your fruit and left your carcass discarded by this road for the scavengers."

Again, his brutish honesty assaulted her, and she flushed. Did he know this was a bluff to draw him in? Was he just playing along to see how far she would go?

The answer didn't matter. In two steps he was across the distance she had thought safe. A strong hand was on hers at the closure of the robe. She nearly swooned. How could she have been taken in so? He had her and quickly. Desperation rode the galloping shiver this time.

His other hand grabbed her left arm through the robe and brutal fingers drove into the soft muscle of her upper arm. His face was close to hers and she felt a stiffness brush her thigh. Her help was not going to make it in time. She almost gave up the ruse by crying out for help. She had teased him into a frenzy, and they would not be able to overcome him. This time she had played it too close and was going to pay for it.

His mouth was open and about to speak when a sharp thud announced the blessed closing of the trap. Her saviors had been able to get into position in time.

The man's grasp on her hand and arm slackened, and he collapsed forward onto her. The stiffness thrust into her soft groin and she exhaled as a shock of pleasure from the accidental invasion rushed up her spine. She cursed herself for feeling anything for such a beast, but he had resisted her more than any man ever had.

"It seems your flower remains unplucked, sister," the brunette holding a mace said. "You are welcome."

"You may chance your virtue next time, sister," she sighed with a mixed feeling of relief and disappointment that she could never admit. "But as we have seen, you do not have the same charm that I do. What is this now, three?"

"You nearly had to give it all away to get this one to bite. Perhaps your age is beginning to reduce your charm."

The allusion did not escape her as she nibbled her lip and considered the young man's potential attentions.

"You like him," the redhead beside her announced with disbelief dripping from her words as she folded the unnecessary net across her arm.

Elsa did not deny the charge, but she was not given the time.

"If he lives, get him in here. I want him secured before we try to find our way back to the village. Perhaps we can convince him to tell us who was so brazen to attack this dowry train. Everyone, even those this deep in the Dragon's Spine knows I'm protected by both my father's house and Price Ardvald's," the princess said from the darkness of the carriage, ending any more play.

GUARDIAN'S AWAKENING

Roark woke with a headache from the blow, bound to the seat, blindfolded, and completely naked. Realization dawned with a shiver, that her recurring nightmare of being discovered hiding as a Guardian was suddenly real. Fear surged, causing a nervous trembling to rush all over the warrior's body, giving away more than she wanted to her captors. She struggled to regain control. She did not want them to know they had an advantage over her. She had to stay strong and ahead of them, and fear was the fastest way to lose.

Once the trembling subsided and Roark's senses started to become more acute, more subtle sensations were trying to cut through the pain and fear.

There was a warm, moist softness brushing her left breast just below her very erect nipple. The smell of rose, lavender, and cinnamon wafted up from the soft cloth. Fear again exploded through her, and the trembling became terrified jerking against the rawhide bonds that she again struggled to control. She refused to scream even though every part of her mind urged her to.

Her greatest fear was upon her. Someone had captured her and realized that she was female instead of the strong male leader she pretended to be. They would soon end these delicate ministrations and start the torment of unending rape. The line of men awaiting their turn would be long. She knew her destiny if she were ever caught. Staying in the village had been no better. The Reeve was no help as he would be the first in line due to his position, so either option ended similarly. She had known since she had first blossomed as a young girl and the leering and touching began that she would always be the prey unless she did something about it. When she had chosen to hide herself among the men she was hiding from, she knew discovery would only make her ultimate punishment worse. Payment for safety over the past few years was now due. She tried to control the trembling as the same warmth brushed her right breast.

Her mind fought with her panic and the sudden hyper sensation that it gave her. Her bare bottom was not sitting on hard wood, but on a delicate silk covering, and it was warm on her recently washed skin. Her bonds were secure but soft on her wrists and ankles. She was warm wherever they had taken her, and it smelled of the oils in the water; water and oils which were caressing both her left and right side. Her mind succumbed to the conflicting information, and she stopped fighting the restraints. This was not exactly what her nightmare had predicted. It was almost enjoyable if it were not a precursor to her nightmare.

"Alexa, Elsa, stop. She is awake and you are obviously scaring her," a soft yet commanding female voice pierced the silence. The darkness remained. Was it possible she was not in the hands of men? She had been... The memory was coming back. The carriage she had rescued from the attacking brigands.

"Where am I?" she croaked against fear and insecurity. She was not gagged, yet. Maybe they wanted to hear her scream.

"You are not what you appear young one. Why do you hide such a beautiful body under such unflattering attire?"

Her secret was exposed, literally. Would the information hurt her more? For some reason, honesty seemed the best course.

"Safety and work. I would find neither in this form in the Spine."

"If you are who I think you are, then you have accomplished much in your male guise. You're a true honor to womanhood." The pride in the stranger's voice was apparent.

"You have me at an extreme disadvantage."

"And you had me in a similar place before my ladies in waiting stopped you. Why did you take my carriage?"

"To save you." Roark had no reason to lie. Not yet. Honesty was keeping her alive and safe for the moment.

"Easy for you to say that, in your position."

Roark did not answer the accusation.

"Are you not the Guardian, Roark, who we were sent to for protection?"

"I am Roark. The other I cannot answer."

A sharp slap on her left breast sent a flash of pain through her side and she could not suppress a gasp. So this was an interrogation, and the punishment was pain. Roark felt more relaxed as her situation became more like her nightmare.

"I do not want to hurt you," the voice seemed to agree with the words, "but I must warn that impudence in your position will not be rewarded. Do you understand?"

"Yes," Roark gritted her teeth suddenly realizing there were other variations of her nightmare she had not considered. She forced herself to be civil. "If I may ask, who I am speaking to?"

"Don't you know already? Weren't you sent to bring us here as prisoners?"

"Sent?" The incredulity in her question did not seem to explain Roark's surprise at the question. "No. I was completing my last contract, and you were there, waiting for me. I had no pre-knowledge of you or who you are. If I had, I would have declined the contract. You're a risk taker who exposes herself to threats she doesn't understand. Your presence is a threat to any caravan you are in. There's not a Guardian I know who would risk their skins to protect your garish advertisement. The corrupt Reeves in this forgotten, uncivilized, badland are more likely to rape you than listen to you. So, whoever sent you this way knew you would never reach the other side of the Spine with your virtue if you somehow made it with your life."

"We were told of the risk before we left."

"Then you proved my original opinion that you are stupid. What you were told is obviously nothing close to the reality. I saved you from a fate you cannot imagine. The only law in the Spine is the sword. None of the realms these passes discharge into dare risk their Men-at-Arms here. If you came here, decorated as bait as you are, without only those dead men and these women to guard you, you are more foolish than I first thought."

This time a sharp slap across her face caused her to flinch and grunt in pain. She could not lie to herself. She was afraid of torture, and the blindness made it even more terrifying. So far, this was mild, but she knew the worst was still to come. What she had not expected was how else the harsh treatment mixed with the mingled softness of the female interrogator made her feel. Part of her wanted to snap off another sarcastic retort to draw another punishment. Part of it was the anticipation. She knew another punishment would come, just not when or where.

A quiet hissing indicated that the mistress was not happy, but Roark could not tell if it was with her answer or the punishment it had elicited.

"My guards take my safety very seriously. You impugn their skills with such comments. We knew this was a risky journey, but it cannot be helped. We must pass this way."

"But you don't have to pass with a sign tacked to your ass that says please rape me and my carriage full of young women."

This time there was a delay before the punishment arrived. Something soft gripped her left nipple and she felt the dual pleasure in both her breast and her loins. Then the pinch grew firmer and pain followed the pleasure. She shivered as it grew intense and a raw groan escaped her unprepared throat. The grip finished with a twist that nearly caused Roark to slide off of the seat if it were not for the restraints.

"Hmm— Finish cleaning her up, and be thorough. I will speak with her more once you have her in a state where she is willing to talk."

The noise of a latch told Roark that they were in the carriage and that someone had exited or wanted her to think they had. As soon as the door closed again the warm towels returned and this time with more vigor and insistence. It was still soft and warm and extremely exciting. Roark felt bad for enjoying the invasion. She wanted to push them away but could not move her arms or legs. She had not realized it before, but soft braces held her legs apart as well as the ties that held her feet to the floor.

She wondered how many men these women had captured this way before and what had happened to them. That made her afraid again of what would happen if she made them angry.

The warm sensation of the towel on her neck was replaced with a hot breath and a gentle nibble. She tingled all over at the sudden competition of sensations.

"Please don't," she whispered as if speaking the words would actually stop the attention.

"Relax and enjoy it. We can show you how," the voice she had confronted outside of the carriage whispered back at her.

"I'm afraid," she admitted to the darkness.

"No need, we mean you no harm." The warm towel circled and teased tender flesh that had recently been sorely treated.

"Then prove it. Stop."

The nibbling on her neck continued up to her ear, and she could smell the rose oil she had smelled before. Warm, soft flesh settled on her left thigh and she knew a naked woman was sitting on her lap. The other woman's breasts rubbed against Roark's taught nipples and she felt her pulse quicken. The nibbling sensation rose along her chin until the soft lips of a young woman lightly caressed hers. Another moan escaped her throat and she felt ashamed that she was enjoying the invasion. If this had been a man she would have screamed against his unwelcome attention, but this was not unpleasant. In fact, it was quite enjoyable and she had not enjoyed a soft embrace in a long time.

"Perhaps if we allowed her to see she would relax," A voice she had not heard on her right seemed to beg in a whimper. The weight on her thigh disappeared and a hand reached behind her head to released the blindfold that had kept her in the dark. A different woman she had never seen before, a younger red head, climbed up to straddle her thigh. Her head descended to nibble on her neck, and Roark could not help but find the younger girl intriguing. She had never been with a woman and she had never really considered it even though she spent most of her time pretending to be male. But, to be fair, none of the caravan women were like this beautiful girl. Roark allowed the young girl to caress her as she looked at the beautiful and clean body. It was a pale color that reminded her of silk she had seen in the cargo of a wagon once, and it was speckled with occasional dark miniature splotches of red that enhanced the stark beauty of the white flesh. Roark was finding her extremely exciting as she looked up at her from her ministrations with a wanting grin.

"I've never been with a Guardian. You will not hurt me will you?"

The sudden juxtaposition of roles shocked Roark as the young girl switched from antagonist to scared supplicant. The surrender was well presented, and if not for the bonds that still held her, Roark almost believed it. There was something bewitching about this young girl. She was winding herself around a place Roark had never knew existed.

Giggles from the other side of the coach reminded Roark that they were not alone. She looked over to see the other two women watching as they embraced in their own caresses.

"Don't mind us," the brunette who had drawn her into the ambush coed quietly at the redhead who had turned her head in a brutal scowl.

"If you trust me," the girl said returning to the submissive role. "I can release these bonds, but you can't run or try to get away. The Princess would be very angry."

"And," Roark croaked before clearing her throat to continue. "I'm sure she's waiting for that very thing so she can cut me down as I try to get away."

She paused and looked around the carriage for the first time. Her fear seemed to dissipate as she looked again into the eyes of the young girl sitting naked in her lap. For some reason the captors were relaxing their grip and allowing her to relax as well. The young woman was giving her a look that said her fears were unfounded and Roark actually believed her. More than that, Roark found herself softening a little in the caresses of this beautiful rose. She nodded at the offer.

"I will not run."

The inside of the carriage was as opulent as the outside. Silk curtains draped over the windows blocking the view in and out. Burgundy leather covered the walls and ceiling. Oil lamps flickered on either side above the back seat where the other two women were embracing one another. The little one worked at her bonds quickly as if there was a reason to hurry, and Roark suddenly realized the woman was excited.

Perhaps she was not pretending her submission and attraction.

Roark was not a virgin. Sex was a tool she used as she needed, but she had never been with another woman. She had never seen the reason. The trains were full of caravan whores who slept with the guards to improve their protection along the way, and several had drawn men from Roark's team away because they had convinced the silly men their spawn was really their own even though there was no way to verify who the father was. Roark had avoided any contact with the caravan women. She could not trust them to keep her secret and giving them that much power over her was not wise. She could say she had never enjoyed sex, and it was always a threat that she would become the play-thing of some brigand, or worse, mother of a caravan brat. She had never considered that she would ever be in a situation like this, and she never imagined that she would enjoy being tied to a bench seat being seduced by another woman.

"What's your name?" Roark asked the girl as she released her second arm. She looked up into her eyes and Roark felt the reality of the girl's desire. The fact that Roark asked her name somehow made it that much more powerful.

"Uhhm," she stuttered, and it made Roark question why. What was so special about her that made this young woman so enthralled by her. "My name is Rowena, but my sisters call me Reva."

"For the mythical huntress?"

"Yes," She smiled up into Roark's eyes with surprise that she would know the legend. It was an eastern myth that did not fare well in the passes where brutal men ruled and broke the spirit of any women who considered being anything but property.

"I hear many things in these trains. The legend of your namesake is shared by many of the young girls who make their way through here." Reva's face mirrored the frown on Roark's face and she continued to explain it. "But, the optimism of the legend is quickly squelched by the brutal reality of these hills. I hope the same does not happen to you."

Roark regretted her words even as she said them because they struck the young woman harder than she had expected. This young one had seen violence and it scared her even now. She continued to stare at Roark, and the Guardian suddenly realized the reason the young one was so enamored with her. She must remind her of someone she had lost. Her throat closed on that realization.

"You're not really related to these other women, are you?"

"None of us are," she whispered as if she was giving away a critical secret. "We come from all over the realms. We're more like you than you know."

"You lost someone you cared for a great deal."

"Yes. You remind me of her. But tell me of your loss. Who did they take from you?"

"My sister," Roark answered in a whisper. "My whole family actually, but I watched my sister die. She was protecting me with her own body. They brutalized her, but they never knew I was hiding in the trunk she was draped over. It was a horrible night."

Roark felt the girl's skin chill at her story. Her muscles turn rigid as she listened to Roark's story that was never shared. With her free hands, Roark drew the woman to her to comfort her.

"We've walked a similar path, perhaps we can walk together for a while?" Roark asked in a whisper.

In that instant, a far more binding contract was signed. Roark knew she would never let the world hurt this one. Roark cursed herself even as she succumbed to the fate she could never deny.

The girl's red head relaxed and nestled into her comforting chest and Roark stroked her hair gently. Together, they comforted each other.

"You intended to protect us, didn't you? Just like you said."

"Yes," Roark answered plainly without releasing her from the embrace.

"I could tell. It was in your eyes. I trust your eyes."

"What does your mistress intend to do with me?"

"She just wants to know the truth about your intentions. It surprised her that you were a woman. She wasn't ready for that, and she doesn't trust anyone."

"Why is she out here? This is no place for her. There is no quarter here for her even if she is royal. No one here swears fealty to any crown. The passes of the Spine are full of the most brutal men in the realms, throw-aways from every realm that touches the foothills. Some are paid by those crowns to keep the borders clear and foreigners out, others just enjoy the sport of it. They will not hesitate. She will be lucky if she is only sold to some pompous prince in the western regions where they treat their women nearly as well as their livestock."

Reva cringed in her arms. "She has already been sold, basically."

"She's on her way to an arranged marriage?"

"The Prince of Parthia. She's promised as a show of the King's interest in peace. Her father's realm has been at war with Parthia for most of his life. You would think the Spine would make that impossible, but both sides seem to manage to strike the other whenever the passes are clear."

Roark nodded and stroked Reva's hair subconsciously. The Princes was doubly cursed. She was a pure woman in the passes where that quality was worth a great deal of money, but more than that, she was a binder on a treaty that no one in the Dragon's Spine wanted to succeed. The financial loss to the Reeves would cripple many of them. Anything that stabilized the passes would hurt the men who lived off of the unstable environment. They helped raid on both sides of the Spine. Roark stroked mindlessly as Reva continued to share more of why the Princess was a double curse and why Roark should have let the brigands have them. Now, she would need to explain to the woman leading this group that she would never survive without Roark's help. And that promised to be more difficult than anything Roark had faced so far. This was turning into a very long day, and Roark was beginning to wonder if she had what it took to do what she knew she had to offer.

~~~

Roark woke again with a start. The coach was empty. She was untied completely from the restraints. She was still naked, and her weapons were nowhere to be seen.

The memory of the young redhead's soft skin against her felt like it had to be a dream, but, everything around her told her it had been real. She was stretched out on the bench seat where she had been tied, and covered with a woven blanket of quality she had not seen on any caravan. The scents of rose, lavender, and cinnamon still lingered. In a moment of lethargy that traveled hand in hand with pleasure, Roark snuggled into the only softness and warmth still around her.

It all tempted her to stay where she was. There was a peacefulness to the quiet roar of the water outside. When it combined with the delicate femininity of the Princess' carriage and the memory of a moment she had never before experienced, it soothed her into a lull that tempted her to sink into the softness and forget the harsh world of the Spine.

Reality snuck into her short fantasy with a shiver. Fear raced over her body. Were they witches? Did they charm her? How would she even know? She shook her head to clear it. She reminded herself that fearful ramblings never solved problems. Everyone knew witches were ugly hags. But, that didn't matter at all. She couldn't stay. The brigands were still out there trying to kill them, and her own men were surely on their way if the brigands weren't.

She threw off the soft cover, discarding the fantasy and the fears together. How long had she slept? Her men were on their way to find her, unless the brigands had prevailed.

This staging area was the fallback point if there were ever to be a problem at the pass stage, and there had been a problem at Spiney Crag. Whoever could would regroup here before continuing with any caravan. Duty was not the best word to use to describe how things worked in the passes of the Spine. The guardians trusted each other and counted on the rules of brotherhood to keep them alive, but there was always the need for a strong hand to keep the brotherhood aligned. The sure knowledge that anyone who broke the trust of it would die kept it stable. Every man under Roark knew that she would fulfill her duty if they failed her, and she was backed up by her First, Malich.

Following the attack, it would take Malich some time to get things under control back in Spiney Crag Gap. Once that was accomplished, he would send a party or more likely lead a party to find her. Finding her like this would damage that trust and brotherhood considerably. Roark knew she was running out of time.

None of them knew the secret she had kept since she joined the ranks of the Guardians. She had maintained it carefully through disguise, careful maintenance of distance, and to some degree luck. Her skill, alignment with a group of strong and reliable fighters, and the deadly nature of the job had catapulted her to leading this band, and, she had to admit, fame. Once she was the leader it was easier, but she needed to keep it that way. If she intended to stay alive she could not be found like this. She was not sure if these women understood how dangerous it was for them if she remained exposed like she was. What her men would do to her, if they knew, was the stuff of her nightmares. She had to get back into her disguise and in control.

She stood as best she could in the low cover of the carriage. Her movements translated to the metal springs and leather strapping that held the coach suspended on the axles. Unavoidable creaks testified that she was up and moving. She looked around the coach again for anything to wear, but her captors had been careful not to leave any tools the warrior could use in easy reach. Frustrated, she grabbed the blanket and threw it around her left shoulder and across herself so that it draped over most of her important features and covered her buttocks. Reasonably covered, she reached for the coach door.

As if they had waited for her to reach for it, the door opened and the party of women entered in a line, forcing her back onto the seat. The youngest girl, the redhead who had so gently manipulated her, grinned at her coquettishly as she sat in the corner farthest away from her.

The brunette who had first distracted her entered next and sat on the seat next to Roark. The final sister, the quiet but apparently calculating middle "sister", entered and positioned herself on Roark's left side effectively blocking her escape.

Their leader entered last and sat down facing Roark. The radiance of her skin and hair, even in the muted light in the carriage, reinforced Roark's first, distant, impression. This woman was as poisonous as a witch's apple to any Guardian who touched her.

No one took any actions to force Roark to do anything more than they already had. No one brandished a weapon even though she knew they were surely present. The leader nodded in a greeting and smiled the relaxed smile of a woman in control.

Roark leaned back against the padded couch. There was no reason to resist yet. It was obvious she wanted to talk. The last encounter had such a different tenor that she was a little concerned with their sudden seriousness. She wrapped her simple cover tighter around herself in an unnecessary show of modesty since there were few secrets between them anymore.

"I see my ladies have done their tasks well. You are not the growling beast we first dragged in here. Although, you seem to have affected my youngest lady somewhat. That is not easy, but be assured that she is your only champion." The Princess paused to let that comment sink in. "Why did you take my carriage, where are we, and where are the rest of my guards?"

Roark, who could see her interrogator this time, stared into the deep blue eyes of the unblemished and untanned face of the young woman. She was amazingly untouched by anything. No woman in the passes had such smooth skin. It looked like fresh cream in a gold rimmed bowl of fine porcelain. She shook her head in momentary disbelief. How could anyone not understand how such a rare commodity would not be harshly sought and taken. She surrendered to the fact that they did not understand and tried to answer the question. With a breath she collected herself. Her host waited with some impatience.

"You misunderstand my intentions. If you will give me a moment to explain, I will start with the simplest answers. I will try to clarify what has happened and what is about to happen."

The lady nodded to her request as was expected from a person of her position. Roark settled a little between her captors as she felt comfortable with her reasons and position.

"Your men, the guards you brought with you and the driver of this coach, are dead," Roark stated so matter-of-factly that the young women-in-waiting inhaled sharply. Their leader did not react. She already knew the most likely outcome of the conflict at the Gap. Roark nodded and moved on. She was not as stupid as he thought she had to be.

"You and your coach were set up. You were marked as soon as you entered that pass town, if not before. I truly believe you were marked before you entered the passes."

Again the princess nodded but said nothing.

"No pass town is safe for such a target as this advertisement of wealth and status. There is too much poverty in the passes for it to go unmolested. That alone, independent of its content proves that whoever made the decision to enter that town the way you did should be lashed in the court until dead if they still breathe. They are complicit in risking your life."

Roark's words struck as they should have. The leader reacted with a slight blush of anger. One negative of such fair skin was the inability to hide reactions like that, but it was not the embarrassed look Roark expected. She had not planned the trip, but she knew who had. Roark made no indication of noticing her reaction and continued.

"The agents who organize caravans in those pass towns are ruthless. None are to be trusted. They adjust to who pays best for what commodity. Quite often they sell a contract for protection of portions of a train knowing it will never make the other side. They get paid by the brigands more than it costs to pay off the contract, and most often the people they owe are dead in the caravan. Do you understand?"

She nodded, unfazed, but still listening.

"You, My Lady, are a commodity of such value in the passes that there is no way you would ever make it to the other side of the passes."

Again she nodded, this time with a look of concern. Something in what Roark had said did not match her own expectation. This was not the first time Roark had briefed someone of her nobility.

"Gaylan, the agent you worked with, however, surprised me. He makes a good cut off of protecting caravans with my troop. He makes enough that it's not worth letting the brigands know about us. Every man has a price, but I had never seen his. Whoever bought him did something impressive. I fear for his family. Either way, he double crossed you. You were sold before I even arrived, and I and my men with you. The brigands who attempted to take your carriage had come to pick up their delivery. They expected to walk in and out without much resistance. If I had not seen you, this would have been far different and far worse for you. I'm sure Gaylan intended to wait until we were in fully. He intended for you to be cut out of the caravan early and with little notice. Your men were dead as soon as they entered that town. You and your ladies were someone else's property already."

"So, you saved us from being taken by taking us yourself?" She asked with a hint of sarcasm that told Roark the Princess partly believed what was being told and was only playing the fool to see what Roark would do.

"You're wasting my time. You know I'm telling the truth. You have since you came back in here. I find your hospitality to be challenging but warm. You know my secret. My men will arrive soon. This adventure will turn bad for us all if they arrive and find me like this. If you know anything about men, you know that I've deceived them. Duty will not survive that slight." Roark took a chance that she could turn this conversation by being the strong leader that she had become in the wilds of the passes.

No one touched her, but Roark suddenly understood the strength of her captor. She changed from a soft and delicate flower of a girl to a suddenly very strong and sharp woman.

"Do not pretend that because I question you now in comfort rather than restraints that you are free. Your freedom is still in question as is my belief. How can I be sure that you aren't here to turn us over to those very brigands you warn us about? As you say, every man has a price, and so does every woman. Gaylan was recommended to us by a reputable merchant. He came highly recommended and my guard checked his reputation before we arrived."

"I'm sure you did, and I'm sure that he checked out better than any other agent in the passes. That is the reason I work with him. As I said, he is the most honest of a bad crowd. There are no honest merchants who work in the passes. They are all party to trading in the suffering of what the kingdoms on either side of the Spine see as the unwanted. The fact that he turned on you tells me that the bounty placed on your head is a life-changing amount. It is probably all he needs to pay off his debt and escape the Spine once and for all. You were his exit price. No man in the pass, no matter his honor, can ignore that opportunity. Like I told you, you were marked as soon as you entered the pass. The news was out on you. You are right to doubt me. If I had been given a similar chance, I probably would have turned you over too."

"You would not," Reva blurted and drew scowls from the other sisters. The Princess actually smiled at the girl's vocal defense and then controlled her reaction by giving her a warning look.

"You still have not told me where you have brought us and what you plan to do with us. How do I know you're not holding me here to collect that very bounty you say you would take?"

"You don't."

She used the honesty to shock the Princess into listening.

"You shouldn't trust anyone in the Spine. I will tell you this. I am the only hope you have of getting through the Spine alive, more than that I can't promise. You have my weapons, my gear, and even my life. You are in control, but let me tell you what will certainly happen next. I have taken you to a location known to my men as a safe haven. It is a place that is difficult to reach except by the road and is surrounded by difficult to climb ridges. Few but those who live in the Spine even know how to get into the ridges and crags around us and those who do have no desire to have you or your gold. It is hard to imagine that a place like this exists in these mountains, and I have worked hard to find places just like it. They make my life easier when I need a place to hide. I pay a high tribute to the people of these ridges to guarantee it. My men will not come up the road, which is why they are not here yet. Anyone who approaches us by the road is the enemy."

She paused to let her points settle a moment. No one challenged her.

"The Brigands who are following you do not know how to get to this place except to follow the tracks and the road. My men will surround this place first, then close in on us to make sure we are safe. The enemy will charge this location because you are three women in a coach protected by a single champion. They lose their advantage by waiting and allowing us to entrench any more than we already have."

Roark looked at her host to measure how the truth was weighing on her. The reaction was calm and accepting, so she continued.

"I brought you here because it was safe, and I could count on keeping you that way until I could figure out what to do. I will need to deal with Gaylan, but before that can happen you have to disappear. You cannot continue in this carriage through this pass. If you wish to survive the pass at all, you have to let me help you disappear into the rest of a caravan, as if you never existed. You and your whole troop must die in the passes today. None can know who you are. My men have probably handled the brigands in the pass. If anyone approaches us from the road we know they are not friends, but we will never stand against them. If, however, my men do what they are supposed to do, we will be surrounded before we even know they are upon us. Use this to decide if you trust me. I know what I'm doing in the passes of the Spine. I know I'm getting into something deep, but it would help me plan this if I knew exactly who you are and why you are in the passes, but first you need to decide if you trust me."

Her hostess paused and looked around at the other women in the coach before she reacted at all. Reva was transparent that she thought she should trust Roark. The other two gave indecisive shrugs.

"So, it seems you want us to believe that you have saved us from a fate worse than death, even though you have no idea of our skills or who we even are. Maybe we had this entire situation under control the entire time. Perhaps we were sent here to draw out those brigands so that the King's guard could take care of them."

Roark smiled a sardonic smile as the woman continued her tale.

"I see that you disbelieve that is possible, but even you were caught by my ladies-in-waiting. They are not without wiles that are useful in these passes. What makes you think we were so much grist for the mill?"

"I admit, my Lady, that you indeed captured me, but it was my desire to protect you that made me vulnerable. If I had been intent upon anything else, you would have failed and this conversation, if it happened at all, would be completely different."

Her forward reaction and honesty seemed to help rather than hurt. The woman considered the situation carefully. The fact that Roark was not still tied to the leather restraints indicated to her that they did not completely distrust her anyway.

"So, why do you fear the arrival of *your* men?"

"Ah, that is the challenge I live with. They trust me as a male warrior, but there is not a man in these passes who believes that a woman can be strong like a man. None would ever follow a woman like me into a battle. Some, thanks to the stories shared in the villages by the surrounding kingdoms, are even superstitious enough to believe that a woman who can fight like me is a witch possessed of demons and here to take their souls like a succubus. I cannot risk letting them think any different. If they find out, I am dead, and you likely follow me."

"You wish to tell me that none of the men in your group know. None of them even suspect?"

"None of them know. My First may suspect, but he is exactly what a First should be. He follows whoever keeps him alive. He doesn't ask questions so long as I keep the men safe, the cargo moving, and the gold flowing. He is not superstitious, in fact he is the best case. He doubts magic in all forms."

"I find it hard to believe that you have kept your secret as well as you think."

"What you may find hard to believe, is that I cannot vouch for how these men will approach you and deal with you if they arrive and I am not clearly in control. They may be overwhelmed with the value of this coach and the women inside it. Independent of who you are, that only makes this worse, you are individually worth a life out of the passes to some of the warlords who live in these mountains. Not just for one of my men. All of them could leave this life for the price you would bring." Roark reinforced her point by rudely pointing and highlighting key anatomical features on the leader. "Your skin alone, so smooth and untouched by the sun and the elements, make you more valuable than you can possibly know. To ask a man to ignore such value is difficult and that is why we must make sure that no one knows that you survived this ride into the wild passes. You have not told me who you are or why you're making this treacherous trek. That is fine, I already have enough information to know how dangerous you are. But, if you wish to survive, you need to trust the guide you came to hire. If you keep secrets from guides you often end up paying for them later, with your life or at least your virtue."

The leader pursed her lips and seemed troubled about sharing the complete truth with Roark. Roark raised her hand to indicate that she not even try.

"Tell me what and when it is important, but think hard about who sent you here and make sure they have no motives that you do not trust. I assume I have not yet proven that I want to help and be your guide. If you are willing to trust me once you see the outcome of my men's arrival, I can get you through the pass. But, I assure you, if my men find me like this, our treatment will not be nearly as enjoyable as you might prefer."

Roark could see the young woman considering everything she had said. She could sense that she was unsure of who to trust as she looked at each of the young women in the carriage. The vote was quick and done without any physical indications.

"Very well, we accept your assistance assuming everything occurs the way you described it." The eldest of the guardians, the brunette who had drawn her in, moved to open the door of the carriage.

"We have things to prepare, I assume. How do you want this to look when the others arrive?"

Roark shifted immediately from her relaxed feminine persona into the male cloak she had worn since she was old enough to understand how to keep men away from her. It was such a visible transformation, that it caused the youngest of the sisters to react.

"Oh, by the forest spirits."

The leader, alarmed by her guard's reaction, looked to the young redhead.

"To survive among these men, I have to trust more than makeup," Roark said in the deeper baritone she used to command. Her voice had an edge to it she had not used in the conversation because it would have thrown her captor's trust a completely different direction, but there was another look in the young girl's eyes. Roark had seen it before from the caravan whores. She was aroused by her male persona. It was an unwanted distraction that Roark pushed off. They had little time until her men descended from the surrounding peaks onto them. She softened her visage only a little to smile at Reva and the young one's eyes betrayed her feelings even more.

Roark moved, realizing this was not the time, and then paused. "I'm going to need to know who you are or at least who you wish to travel as. We were never formally introduced."

"Ah, yes. I am Princess Cinnia of Arandor, this in my private guard." She pointed to the senior of the three as she began introductions. "You met Elsa, who is quite a good distraction. This is her sister Alexa." The Princess pointed to the blonde and then to the redhead, "and this young woman who needs to get her passions under control because she is somewhat smitten by you is Reva, the youngest and most nimble of our team. She is our scout. She is quite good at getting into, and out of, places others cannot."

The young girl brightened at the compliment. Apparently, she was not used to being the center of attention. Roark would have to manage her reaction, or Reva would get her killed. For some reasons the young vixen had her heart and the worst of it was that she knew it. Roark nodded to each of them.

"Very well, thank you for trusting me. Where are my things?"

Reva pointed out of the carriage to a chest that had been taken down from the back storage. The young girl, who more and more reminded the Guardian of her namesake in her fox-like moves and mannerisms, pulled a key from a small pouch that was hidden artfully in the folds of her dress and handed it to Roark. The warrior paused as she took the key, remembering the softness and beautiful opalescence of her skin.

"You will find everything there," the quiet soprano fluttering in her voice reminded Roark of the promising whispers and how close they had been. Roark could not allow this to continue. She had to get control of her emotions. She had never felt this way toward anyone.

"Thank..." the words died in the brief explosion of a physical shiver that rushed up her arm and down her back as their hands touched with the transfer of the key. Reva was not unaware of the reaction. Her eyes caught Roark's and the surrender in them again promised more when they could get together. Roark knew that her own eyes were promising something similar, but she also knew that her tough facade was failing around this tempting fox. She took the key and turned to exit the carriage. She paused to stare at the chest where her things were locked away. She would need to keep this young girl close to her or very far away. As she stared at the simple chest holding the dirty rags and deceptive components of her male persona, Roark was not sure which choice would be the safer for both of them.

GUARDIAN'S ADVANCE

While Roark had been held in the carriage, the Princess' ladies had been busy. They had pulled a small tent from the cargo box and set up a travel kitchen that had supported the entire contingent as well as the private guard that traveled in the carriage with her.

A fire was gradually roasting a pair of recently killed hares while a pot boiled to bring dried vegetables back to an edible state. Roark stifled a comment on how well they ate on their travels as she thought of some of the caravan families who shared a mutton thigh bone to season their weak soup that became more and more watery every day. She was back in her male clothes and fidgeting at several things she worried didn't look just right anymore. Her big problem was that she was never seen around women in the caravan, and now she was surrounded by them. In this crowd of beautiful women, there was too much opportunity to compare her and see the flaws in her disguise. She wanted to crawl into a hole. Being around the other women made her feel her true self, and that made her unsure she was still able to hold her life saving appearance. The sun was setting behind the high ridges that surrounded them.

Roark felt a twinge at the base of her neck. Someone was watching her. She held her gaze on the fire as she tested the air and took in the entire situation. There was no reason to let the watcher know that she knew they were there. She had just pinpointed the location of the watcher to her right side when Reva joined her. In a flash of recognition, the girl drew a dagger from her belt and began to move into a defensive crouch.

"Hold. Do not react to them," Roark whispered as he grabbed the young girl's hand and drew her into her side. As if she knew Roark's intentions, Reva sat down next to her and laughed as if they had just shared a joke. Roark cringed. Attempts to hide actions often came across as too broad sweeping, but Reva pulled off her light touch and even Roark wanted to believe they were sharing a humorous moment around the fire. She carefully took the dagger from the girl and placed it in her lap. She took up a stick and ministered to the fire. Her search for the others was skillful. She looked without looking, scanned the surroundings with what seemed only passing interest. Roark was impressed. Only he knew when she had found the watcher.

She followed Reva's example. She needed to know if these were her men. She was waiting for some sign of identification and if it didn't come soon, she would have to react before they were surrounded.

The other women had picked up on it now. The noise from the kitchen tent had become a little subdued but not so much that their watchers could tell. It was more of a feeling. The entire camp was suddenly aware but not reacting. Elsa and Alexa had moved closer to their own weapons and shifted out of the cover to where they could see better. The sands in the glass were running short. Soon, someone would make a mistake and a fight would break out.

Roark's bow was lost in the fight to get the carriage away. There was no sentimental value to it, but she would have liked to have it as whoever was circling them now closed the noose. She inwardly cursed at how these women had relaxed her too much. She was soft when she shouldn't be, and now they were caught. Mistakes like that would get them all killed. Reva gave her an understanding glance and Roark was again impressed with the young woman's skills and how they were starting to establish the type of unspoken understanding that warriors developed only after years of working together. She looked toward a space across the fire which was protected from the position on the ridge above them where they knew one of their pursuers was watching. Reva's simple look and Roark's nod established the agreement that she should move when the sign came.

A quiet trill of a patchwren echoed from the peak to her left and Roark immediately gave the recognition signal in answer. She also gave Reva a cautioning hand signal to let her know this was expected. The trilling call and answer would have vanished into the other noise of the forest if the entire camp had not been awaiting the first actions of battle. The tension that had descended from the ridgeline surrounding them amplified as Roark's First stepped out onto the road they had followed to get to the staging area.

Roark stood to give her second-in-command an additional signal indicating everything was fine while signaling to the other ladies to wait. Twenty men stepped from the surrounding foliage and edges. She and Malich moved together and met in the road. Her First raised a cluster of items that she had abandoned as she had raced to save the coach from the brigands. Among them was her bow and quiver.

The sign of the tools being returned to her made up her mind. As her hand wrapped around the riser and gripped the smooth wood, Roark transitioned from standing to kneeling, dropped everything else except the bow, pivoted around in an arc, nocked an arrow in her bow, drew to her ear, and released.

The arrow flew toward the position where the scout who had given away the team's approach was still standing. The razor sharp point sliced across the scouts cheek and ear cutting a gash in the delicate skin and cartilage but otherwise leaving the man unmarked. The scout reacted to the injury by bringing his hand up to the now bleeding cuts. He had not even seen Roark move once Malich had passed her the bow. It was a sad sign when Roark could mark a man so easily. She questioned now if she should send another arrow directly behind it to save herself trouble in the future. She stood to her full height dropping the bow to her side and looked at her First.

"Anyone who gives away the team's position dies out here. These women knew you were upon us. If I had allowed it, they would have fought you even to this little one, or escaped like the fox into the surrounding cover. Even though you had been mostly successful in closing the trap. It only takes one mindless oaf to destroy your hard work." Roark turned in a circle to make sure her voice was heard by all of her men and finally faced her First again. "You will train that one. I marked him for you. He will be easy to identify if he chooses to continue to skulk about. If he doesn't all the better."

"Aye, that one will spend some time under my boot. He's young, stupid, and 'ill be sorry for his lapse. Don' doubt it Roark," her First replied as if they had been in full agreement on the scout's punishment all along. Roark thought nothing more of the issue.

"Took you a while to get here, Malich. Did you get the caravan in safely without me?"

"Aye, credits ar'n our account, but Gaylan's a nervous mother waitin' for word o' his lost gem." Malich pointed at the coach with a look that gave Roark a complete understanding of Malich's opinion of the gilded target.

"You mean he's nervous he's lost his bounty. The bastard set us up."

"Aye, you don' ha' ta' tell me he's dirty this time. I got an eye on him." He frowned at her scornful look. "A better eye 'an tha' one I tell ya'"

Roark returned his grin letting her first off of the hook for the scout's poor performance. It happened and lessons had to be taught.

"He's hurt us before as we've thought, but this one will get us dead, I'm afraid," Roark settled into the easy banter that had developed between her and Malich over years of working together.

"If we take it the way it looks, but ya' don' mean to be that daft do ya'?"

Roark smiled a broad smile at her First. "I'm glad we still think so much alike. It would be hard to be this right without you being beside me."

Reva appeared at Roark's side. The Guardian could sense the sudden jealous energy surrounding the young woman. It was a dangerous sign and it could undo all of her years of trust building. She was sure Malich would sense it if she didn't distract him, so she reached out and grabbed the girl around the waist and drug her over to her side roughly in a one arm embrace common among men who owned women.

"I may have to thank the cheating bastard for this one though." She kissed the young girl roughly and looked around at the somewhat shocked faces of Reva's protective sisters. Roark could not have coached a better reaction. Elsa was gripping the hilt of a dagger at her side tightly and staring at Roark as if she intended to drive the blade into her back. It was nothing like the look Reva was giving her even though the brutal kiss was itself hard not to enjoy. Feeling the girl's soft skin against her even for the brief instant was exciting. She was sad that the young one had let her emotions cloud what was developing between them. She should have read the move and played into it. They were still getting used to each other.

"Ya say. I've never seen ya take to caravan whores, but maybe ya found ya one meets your standards. I'll 'ave ta pay up if it's true," Malich grinned at his leader and took in the other two women, "and you've cost me dearly," he said with a grin at the redhead. "But it makes sense, ya 'ave high standards, boss. Ain't all though. We saw the other, and tha's what makes this un tough, eh?"

"It is. She's in the coach."

"It's as bad as it gets, eh?"

"Aye. Worse."

Malich stepped into the ring surrounding the fire and looked his leader directly into the face. "I think the boys're nervous 'bout this un. I lost some a the new blood on the way, the ones who survived."

Roark flinched at the news that there had been losses in the fight. She had hoped they were better trained.

"It was a heavy force then?"

Malich nodded.

"They should be nervous. Do we have a problem?"

"Na, those who're with ya, are with ya no matter the treachery. There's always loss in tha pups. Their loss, not ours. They can crawl back to their ma's tit, sure."

Malich and Roark smiled together. Roark released Reva to return to what she was doing with a harsh swat on her ass and grabbed Malich's wrist in a strong grasp. They shook briefly grasping each other's wrist and Roark pulled Malich toward him and embraced her First in a one arm greeting.

"You did right, Malich. You read this one right," Roark spoke in tones that were restricted to only those around the fire. "We'll have to hide this group among the caravan to save it and ourselves. None outside this group, and I question if we can trust that much, can know who they are. You brought the closest ones with you? None you don't trust?" Roark tilted her head toward the scout with the marked ear as an example.

"He's new an' hungry. He made a mistake. He'll learn. Ya could 'ave killed 'im, an he knows it. These are the core. We can trust 'em. The lost ones were buffer in case we 'ad a fight awaitn'."

"I trust you to make sure. They have to know I saved them today by dragging this mess into the forest. Spread some silver among them. Remind them that we pay for the risks."

"Done afore we left tha' stinkin' town."

Roark nodded. "Gaylan has to think they're dead. Everyone has to think this ended badly for us."

"Then we'll make 'im think just tha'. Tha' means you can' come back with us. You hav' ta meet up with us in the pass. We'll return withou' ya."

Roark realized at that moment that he and Malich were two of a kind. The way the man followed even unspoken orders made her proud. For a moment, while she considered his comment about paying up, she wondered if he already knew her secret and was keeping it for her. How could they be this close and him not know? It was an uncomfortable moment that she tried to hide in a strong manly pounding on her First's shoulder. Their eyes met. The trust between them had never been broken since they had joined the caravan circuit together. She knew he had her back no matter if he knew or not.

"Glad you made it through that trap. Glad you're the one who made it here. I need the best on this one."

"Aye, an' y'll 'ave it. Ya gonna tell 'em 'ow ta dress. This won' work at all. Ya gonna 'elp 'em look right?"

Roark looked at Malich to see if there was more to his question and then moved on without answering.

"We need a wagon. Can you leave part of this crew with me or will Gaylan notice the difference?"

"If ya' get 'em to the first stop from 'ere on foot, we'll 'ave a wagon. 'ow're we 'andlin' the cost if Gaylan think's 'em dead?"

"They'll contract with us directly. I think I can work that out."

Her First nodded understanding and looked at the gear and carriage. "Shame ta waste it?"

"How thorough do you think Gaylan will be in investigating? Will he send men out to check this?"

Malich nodded. "Aye, someone'll send a band out. Maybe not Gaylan. May 'ave already. They'll not trust our word. If'n he's ina this as far as ya think. I'm more worried 'bout the man who paid 'im."

Malich voiced the unspoken concern. Roark could deal with Gaylan's treachery. That man was transparent, but this situation might draw out the men behind it all. Were they ready for that?

"Then we have to make it look real," she said, letting her concerns fill those words.

"Aye," her First replied with equally deep feeling in very few words.

That conversation decided it for them, and Roark knew what had to happen in order to save the lives of the women in the carriage.

"Time is short, let's get started. Hand pick me a team of five that you trust with your life. Can you spare that many?"

"Brought 'em just in case, boss." Malich grinned at having matched his leader's plan so well.

"Not that one?" Roark questioned knowing the answer to lighten the mood. Her First feigned a hurt look, and Roark smiled.

Roark clapped him on the shoulder again in appreciation of their working relationship, then turned toward the carriage and the preparations that had to be made. The show would not be hard, but hiding a pearl like the one hidden inside amongst the dregs of a caravan would be nearly impossible. They would have to trust her, and Roark was not yet sure that they did.

~~~

Roark cracked the carriage whip in the air above the heads of the team, and the blindfolded horses responded immediately. Muscles in their backs rippled in unison as they dragged the heavy carriage forward in jerking starts. It was a lighter load than it had been. Her men had harvested portions of the gilding, partly to pay for the supplies for the upcoming journey, but equally just because it was a shame to leave it. She was sure someone had already stamped it out into scales, the local name for gold and silver hand stamped for use as currency in the Spine.

As the team of prized Kalians synchronized their efforts and pulled forward slowly, Roark aimed and struck the whip again. The lead horse shivered and shook her blindfolded head with a snort of complaint at the rough treatment but increased her speed all the same. The other horses followed with chuffing acceptance, reminding Roark that the team worked and suffered together. In a short distance, they were pulling the carriage at a respectable speed.

Standing atop the tall wagon as it bucked and rolled, Roark could not suppress a shiver of doubt that she might not even survive the high-risk maneuver that she had conceived. It was important that the accident look real, and someone had to guide the team right to the edge or they would stop even though blindfolded. The team's belief that the driver knew what was happening was required to send them over the edge. For a brief moment, she felt remorse at having to destroy such beautiful horses— prizes of the Kalian Steppes. Then she focused on what she had to do.

In her feet, she could feel the speed was not right yet. With another whip crack to the magnificent haunches of the lead horse, she urged the team to a faster cadence in the short stretch leading to the bridge.

The speed of the team and carriage increased quickly as the horses understood the desire of the teamster and accepted that she knew where they were going.

The carriage was at full speed as the turn approached. The falls on the right cascaded down in a misty spray that washed across the bridge next to the pool. To the left, the torrent that was contained for only a moment in the pool continued to fall across numerous rocky outcroppings that created rainbow-casting misty halos of their own, disguising the promised death in colorful obscurity. Navigating a team through the turn would be hard at a slow speed, but she needed this to look like a mistake had been made as the panicked driver had rushed to escape. This needed to look real. She lined the team up just off of the center of the bridge. She had only seconds to escape sure death.

Roark looked into that glistening mist for her tightly timed escape. She knew it was hanging exactly in line with their current path, but the rope remained invisible against the dazzling fog.

Doubt tried to distract and kill her. She had to trust that it was where she had placed it. She had to believe that she would be able to hold on to the rope that was surely soaked. In a final thought before it was too late, she reminded herself that it didn't matter. She was committed now. There was no opportunity to change course. If it wasn't there, or if she missed it, she would die with the team of horses at the bottom of the gorge.

In one final push to guarantee success, she urged the team to a frenzy with one last command, stood in the driver's seat, and grabbed for the rope just as it appeared exactly where it was supposed to be. With a final leap and a strong pull, she was free and clear of the hurtling mass of animal flesh and wood. The lead horse was off target to make it across the bridge. The harness just cleared the rail of the bridge as the lead horse reached out and found no ground. Her reaction of panic reached the others, but it was too late. The second horse in the line was already in the air before the panic from the lead horse reached her. With two horses out of control and falling, the other horses started to panic and rear in the harness, and with the slick bridge making it impossible for any change, the whole mass of horses and carriage suddenly pivoted and lurched over the edge, ripping the railing of the bridge away with it. The carriage plunged into the deep cleft around the falls, following the now fully terrified horses.

Roark looked away from her particularly good view of the gorge as the horses and carriage crashed into the first rainbow haloed outcropping. Using skills learned in the caravans she closed her mind to the sound of the crash and the suffering of the animals as they fulfilled their duty to protect the Princess and her ladies. She knew their suffering would be over soon. The first outcropping was not the last one before the whole mess, or as much as made it that far, would finally fall into the churning pool below. It was an unfortunate waste of valuable animals, but the accident had to look real.

Even though she expected it, the lurch of the rope she clung to alarmed her as one of her men released her back to the lip of the trail. Her hands slipped against the wet hemp but held until she was lowered to the edge of the bridge. She carefully stepped onto the path. The bridge could not be trusted. With a quick look down into the cleft of the valley, she grinned satisfactorily then walked back to join the Princess and her retinue.

Their change in appearance had been inaugurated and Roark was glad to see them beginning to appear less like women of privilege and at least somewhat more like caravan women. It might just save them yet.

As she walked up to them, she saw the masked shock of realization on their faces. Reva, who was failing the most to hide her shock, looked at her with an unmistakable twinge of hate. Roark felt a shiver of pain at the loss of some guarded innocence and perhaps the blossoming partnership she had sensed the night before. Reva was the youngest, and the brutal reality was hitting her hardest. In a soft moment, one she would have warned anyone else against, Roark wanted to pull the sweet girl to her for comfort. She missed the submissive eyes and almost loving glances. With an effort of will Roark suppressed the emotion. She could not allow her edge to dull again. Not now. All of them were counting on her.

The Princess stood stoically and showed no sign that they had just forced a team of horses to plunge to their own deaths chased by the crushing weight of their load. Roark tried again to settle herself, to fight off the urge to comfort.

Unable to resist and unwilling to listen to the warnings in her mind, Roark reached out and stroked the young girl's cheek with her thumb as she lifted her sagging chin so that their eyes met. The horror and growing hate in those eyes nearly crushed the stronger guardian's fortitude. If she didn't do something to bring her back from this shock, her instability on the team would be a risk.

"They gave their lives to save you, don't make their sacrifice meaningless," she whispered trying to soften the situation.

The girl could not react. It was all too fresh in her mind and the perceived betrayal the night before was too fresh. Roark may have made a mistake in treating her harshly, but she had to protect her appearance in front of her First. For another aching moment, Roark wanted to hold the woman in her arms and protect her from what was coming. It was going to get worse. Perhaps some day in the future, beyond the threat that loomed all around them, that would be possible again, but first they had ground to cover to make the animals' sacrifice worthwhile.

Roark let the pain fall from her shoulders. She had to move on. She stepped away from that hopeful promise of someday, back into the real world where they were being chased by brigands, and inspected the work they had done to conceal the richness and beauty of each woman. They each now wore rags compared to the dresses they often chose. Elsa was dressed, like her sisters, in a recently stained peasant blouse that covered her fully. A functional woolen tunic laid baggily on top of it. Very little color covered what Roark knew was a most inviting bosom. A functional belt at her waist provided a place for some of her possessions, but what did not fit there was stored in a bundle pack that she carried over her shoulders. The rest of their possessions were at the bottom of the drop with the shattered carriage. It had to look as real as possible. Reva, who had taken personal charge of her own transformation looked less like a waif and more like a female version of one of the Guardians. Roark had allowed her the room to explore her character and it had an interesting affect. Her First had noted the difference and gave Roark an eye as they had emerged from their tents. She had nodded back and given him a sign that they had time to work it out. Her First shook his head and arched an eyebrow. Roark knew the look. Malich had given it to more than one young recruit who was letting a piece along the trail have control. Roark nodded back that she understood the risk and owned it. He gave her the same disappointed look he would give the recruit.

The three sisters, who had experience looking a part, had little problem descending into their dirty roles. Elsa and Alexa had relished the application of the dirt to their faces and what little exposed skin showed. They were getting into their roles.

Reva's refusal to wear a long skirt because it made it hard for her to scout ahead for them now placed her in a different role. Roark planned to give her the chance she was asking for and make her a part of the guards. There was nothing Roark could do about the anger the girl felt right now. If Reva was professional, she would work it out. If not, Roark would deal with it later. She had decided to use Reva's age to their advantage. Roark's vision may have been off or somewhat biased by her charm, but she was having a hard time seeing the young woman anymore. Reva was suddenly doing a passing job of looking like a young man. Somehow, she had used her anger and it was shaping her jawline slightly different.

Her lack of experience as a scout in the passes might make her a risk, but Roark maintained hope that Cinnia's opinion of her would show through as they made their trek by foot to the next stage. So far, the little fox had shown promise.

Cinnia, the Princess of Arandor, was another challenge entirely. Even covered in dirt and dressed in rags of a matron leading her daughters on the dangerous crossing, the woman shone like new brass. Roark continued to see little signs that even an unexperienced hunter would certainly see. Any of those hints of civilization out here would give them all away.

"My lady. I realize this is going to be hard. As we make progress today, this will become easier for you because you will be tired, but you must relax your posture. I need for you to slump like the hard-worked woman you are pretending to be. Your posture breaks the illusion and puts us all at risk."

It amazed Roark that the woman who was used to being taken care of and treated as her station deserved was even able to consider descending to this level. Roark had been direct with her. She told her that this was the only way they would survive, and even this was no guarantee. The more bedraggled and worn they looked the less attention they would attract. The reality of the caravan was that even disguising them as they had would only reduce the risk. Other men and even other women would figure out their secret. And, if they didn't, women traveling alone in the caravan often had to give themselves to a guard to guarantee safety.

Roark hoped the two days of overland travel ahead of them would dull the edges of difference, and she had assigned a male companion for each to act as if they had already established the required relationship. Each man was solely responsible for their charge and paid handsomely to keep their hands to or on themselves. She had reserved Reva for herself and no one questioned the choice, but her change in appearance was good enough that Roark had to change how she acted toward her.

Roark had assigned herself the Princess as well. It was probably too much to take on both, but she had to remember that her job was to protect the Princess. Reva, if she was being honest, was her choice, because she obviously felt something for the sprite, but even that had to come second to the mission. She hesitated to call the feeling she had love. They had just met, but she found herself worrying for the elvish girl's safety. She knew about familiarity attachments and the attraction that could grow between two people who shared some intimacy, as they had, even though it had been somewhat forced. It could create a connection. Roark had never connected with any one like she did with the young redhead. Malich was the closest she had ever come, and their relationship was completely professional. Her lack of connection with other people was the cause, or at least the excuse she had always used, for her perceived harshness. It was also creating a risk Roark had never dealt with. For the first time, she had a handle that someone could manipulate.

"Let's get moving," she called to break out of the thoughts that were threatening to overcome her composure. She had to gain some control of the wandering of her mind about the youngest one. She needed perspective.

"We have a long way to go and it's not getting any shorter," she said. She clapped Malich on the shoulder in a terse goodbye. He would take the others back to the caravan while Roark worked his way around to meet them. Malich grunted as he took the load of responsibility again and walked away.

Her men moved into their protective ring. Two men took a position behind Roark on both sides. Two more created a box around the women. The last man slid back to keep an eye on the back trail. Roark stepped forward to take the point of the ring. Within the ring the women organized into their own protective triangle. Reva was forward as their scout and Elsa and Alexa flanked the Princess. Any skilled brigand would see the defensive patterns, but that might help them run off the most dangerous. Maybe their appearance of strength would protect them.

"Reva," Roark called back over her shoulder. The still somewhat shocked young woman reacted slowly but eventually walked up to join her. When they were shoulder to shoulder, she smiled at the girl to let her know that she was doing well. The feminine side breached her facade for just a moment and the girl's appearance also visibly shifted. As the glance extended until Reva looked away with a coquettish giggle, they had both softened. Roark pushed aside a spark of hope that she had not destroyed any possibility that the girl shared her feelings. It seemed impossible that they could connect in such a short time and in such a dangerous way. There was a sliver of civility in the brutal wilderness, and Roark found herself yearning for it. She had never felt this way about anyone, how could she feel so connected to this girl?

As they walked together, Roark attempted to repair any damage she had caused to their relationship. It felt odd that she wanted to do anything at all, but this was new territory for her. She had to be careful and make it look like she was teaching because her own cover was at risk as well.

"I want you to know, I do what I must to protect us all. My cover, our cover, this facade you and I are putting on, is our only hope," she whispered as she started training the young girl. She hoped it was enough. "As a scout," she continued more loudly for the others. "I need for you to keep me aware of what's ahead of us. Can you do that? Can I rely on you? Can you get ahead of us stealthily and tell me what's ahead?"

The young girl gave her a defiant look as if her very existence had been questioned. They were far enough ahead of everyone except the man walking point that Roark considered it possible to talk without being overheard.

"You're mad at me," Roark said avoiding the dance of denial. "I treated you roughly. That shocked you. I had to. I can't let my men think I'm weak. They expect me to act a certain way. They can't know I'm not what they think I am. Can you understand?"

Reva nodded and Roark could see that her decision to explain was helping. She also felt a little better for having explained. This pixie of a woman was charming Roark. She knew it. She hated it. She also knew there was nothing more she could do about it now. There was something about the way she had looked at her, trusted her, and even caressed her that she could not get out of her mind. She longed for her touch, soft and warm on her neck, on her breast— Roark shook her head to clear the thoughts of their last encounter and focus on their surroundings. For a moment she wondered if the vixen was hexing her as they walked together.

"Would it be easier to hide us among your men, like you hide now? Maybe hiding us as women is more dangerous than you think," the girl offered nervously.

Roark considered her thought. When she didn't answer, the young girl seemed to shrink but said nothing.

"I'm considering what you said," Roark said as she realized Reva thought her silence was resistance. "Tell me more."

"You're not the only one who can disguise herself as a man. We have all played parts when necessary that were not natural for us. If we just looked like a group of guards in the caravan, we would blend in better. We could stay closer to our guards. If we show up already looking the part, there will be fewer questions. Look at me as an example. I'm sure my sisters can do the same. And, perhaps you have not considered how you will explain returning with four women in tow. Where did we come from?"

Roark had not considered that option, partly because it might expose them, and her to danger. But they were all in danger anyway. Her idea had merit, and she was right about the questions. She had been working on how to solve that already.

"Are the others willing?"

"They were willing to let you dress them as caravan whores."

Roark suddenly realized that she had marked them that way by dressing them and making them stay close to the guards.

"When we stop this evening, we will adjust. Now, are we okay? Do you understand why I had to do what I did?"

"You should not wait. The longer we travel like this, the more likely we will be seen like this," she paused to consider the other question. "I guess I understood all along, you just surprised me. It was shocking to see you be so much like a man. I-I was not expecting it." The girl paused and looked at her boots. "It was actually exciting, in a way," she whispered as if saying it aloud would get her punished. The girl looked up after a moment and a shy smile crossed her lips. The sparkle in her eyes showed that she was telling the truth. A delicate breath escaped her throat as she continued. "I enjoyed being in control when we first met." She blushed beneath the dirt. "Torturing you as a brigand was exciting, but I admit I liked it more when you're in control. There's something about you. You lead naturally."

Without another look the girl trotted ahead of the group leaving Roark to consider what the vixen had said. It was as if she had slapped her with an open hand. When her eyes and mind cleared from the emotions left in the girl's wake she saw a completely different image. She suddenly looked like a teenage boy frolicking in front of the party without a care or concern about her safety, but Roark could see the times when the girl checked the trail ahead and noted concerns back to her. Roark realized she had not considered the Princess' ladies as an asset. That would change, by the time they joined the caravan, they would look like a recruitment train. Roark allowed herself a relaxed chuckle. They might even pull this off. If everything worked just right, they might survive to see the other side of the pass, and she might even owe it all to the red-fox, Reva, namesake of the mythical fairy herself.

GUARDIAN'S DECEPTION

It had taken less time to convince the Princess and her ladies to change their appearance than it took to actually accomplish the transformation, primarily because they had to do it all themselves. Roark could not help them without giving away a secret she would prefer to keep. Even after her encounter with the Princes and Reva the idea of being exposed to her own men and others made her shiver.

After Roark had agreed that Reva's idea was sound, they had talked to the Princess as they had walked. They immediately started adjusting with what resources they had. To the men of the company, it appeared that the Princess and her ladies had slowly transformed along the road.

Hair was the least of their challenges because most of the male guards had long hair. Roark's men all matched her appearance, forced by her First, and wore no beards except for what grew between opportunities to shave. Some of the men that had been with her the longest even shaved daily on the trail. She had heard, as she walked the ranks, that the challenge of keeping a blade keen enough to shave with was a sign of skill as was shaving without cutting themselves up too badly. This made it possible for the ladies to get away with makeup that made them appear to have stubble but no beards. By the time they made camp for the night they were mostly there. The next day was for final touches and checks of appearance on the trail. By the end of their second day, Reva's plan was complete, and the party had changed into a recruiting party.

"Boss, I understand the idea, but do they really think they're going to fool anyone?" Jarvi, the senior of the team her First had left behind, asked when they set up camp for the second night.

Roark wanted to laugh at her soldiers. Because they had watched the transformation happen, it was hard for them not to see the beautiful women they had guarded. But her trained eye, the one she used to make sure she looked her part, was impressed. The Princess had been the hardest with her complexion, figure, and hair; but Reva and Elsa had worked most of the day making changes until the right combination of bulk, armor, styling, and dirt had transformed her. She could never speak, but that was not hard when she was expected to be a warrior. Alexa provided the solution for that with some very convincing makeup applied on her neck to give it the appearance that an injury at youth had taken her voice. The maintenance of that appearance would take time each day—Roark knew all about that—but it could be done. With the right separation from the rest of the caravan, she felt they might just make it work.

"Wait until we meet the others," she assured him. "Act like nothing is different, make sure the other men do the same. You may be surprised. We may even fool most of our own men, but that requires you and your men act like they are recruits and not women."

Jarvi raised an eyebrow and shook his head in disbelief, "But, boss, ya can' 'spect us ta treat 'em tha' way…"

Roark's severe look shut down the protest.

"Aye. We'll see, boss. I still don' see it."

"You and the other's just cover their backs when we get into a fight. They can handle themselves, but they're still expecting us to protect them."

"Don' ya mean if we get in'a fight?"

"No. You know we can't avoid fights on a regular day in the passes, this will be even worse."

"Then ya don' think they's gonna' believe they's dead," Jarvi said more than asked.

"No."

The fifteen-year-old who had joined Roark's teams from one of the southern pass villages nodded, grunted, and turned back to his tasks of setting up the guard rotations. He didn't believe there would be no fight either.

Roark didn't think they would face a fight that night, but she never knew. As the boy faded into the dark surroundings, a figure Roark was becoming very familiar with dislodged from a tree and slipped over to her side. She had gone to being away from the group all the time and only reporting in when she had news. In most cases she was never seen with the party at all.

"We're being followed," Reva said as quietly as she could.

Roark simply nodded.

"It's a small party and they're tracking us not shadowing us."

The girl was a good scout, she knew the difference, and that difference helped them. If they were tracking them, they knew how many but not what their makeup was exactly. A good tracker might even know that, but it didn't matter. Roark knew this would turn into a fight before it was settled. It was just a matter of controlling where that fight happened.

"Are you able to distract them?"

"Some, but they are good and seem to have some sense of where we're going."

That was bad news. Roark chewed on what it meant for a moment.

"That probably means one of my men is helping them."

Roark couldn't see the girl's reaction be she knew she was surprised.

"Whoever it is will go out to meet them tonight while we rest." The hairs on Roark's neck tingled as they raised through the sweat of the heavy gear. She hated the idea that one of her's was a spy, but she knew it had to be. No group in the passes could ever be pure. There was too much opportunity for corruption. All you could do when you found it was apply the worst penalty, then the others knew what the cost was.

"Tell your sisters. Set up a rotation to make sure the watchers are watched, and find my spy."

Roark felt the nod more than saw it as the girl stepped into the darker surroundings. She felt bad about putting the ladies at risk, but they were the Princess' final guards. They knew what they had to do. They had all sworn their oaths before they left on this journey.

The guards were setting up their watches. Roark would stand one of them just like the other men. She made sure everyone in her unit pulled duty and shared in the work. It made her job a little harder now because she would have to stay up most of the night to make sure they were safe, but this was not the first time she had gone without sleep. To fight off the fatigue, she found a small pouch on her belt with her left hand and pulled out a pinch of black fungus, Night Warden, from the organized collection of herbs and natural unguents she kept stocked for these very needs. She kept that pouch full and replenished the dried lichen whenever she could find it on the trail.

The other pouches held a combination of rolled leaves, pellets of herbs, and fibrous patches of moss that had equally important effects. She pinched the mass together between her fingers and slid it between her cheek and gum on the side of her mouth. It took very little time to feel the results. A flush of warmth ran over her limbs and her heart rate increased. She called it by the name she preferred because it matched her use. It was known for other outcomes as well. Any feeling of fatigue rushed away. She had used this and other secrets of the herbalist and apothecary to her advantage in many situations. She would not need to rest tonight. She might even be able to extend that into a couple of nights if she were careful, but after that she would have to rest.

Reva was beside her again. Roark felt her arrive and had to suppress an urge to draw a dagger in defense. The girl's skills were quite good. Roark did her best to suppress her reaction, but the grin on the girl's face told her that she failed.

"They are prepared to watch. The Princess is resting as are they. As the night deepens they will watch for signs. I'm going to keep vigil."

Roark dipped her fingers into her pouch again and pulled out another pinch of the dried mushroom.

"Here, place this in your cheek and leave it there."

Reva looked at the dark bunch and then looked up at Roark, "You're not trying to take advantage of me are you, sir?" she asked in her playful way.

Roark felt the enhanced circulation in her body jolt with the sudden memory of the girl's naked body rubbing against hers. She had to be careful and remain focused.

"If the situation was not so dire, yes, but this evening we must remain vigilant."

"You know that's Maiden's Bane you're offering me? What else should I think?"

"Yes, in stronger doses it reduces inhibition, induces hallucinations, and creates a substantial increase of sensitivity. In this small dose, it only provides an increase in energy and enhanced senses."

"So, you have a lot of experience with this?"

Roark could hear the humor in the girls voice even though her face remained stoic.

"Some, but not like you think. I don't use herbals that I don't understand. In my village this was often used for many purposes. We call it Night Warden. Used correctly, mixed with another herb, it can even help extract the truth from someone."

"Hmmm," the girl replied.

"I'm not trying to drug you, I promise," she commented and then added, "well, not more than to keep you awake and attentive."

Reva took the pinch of mushroom and placed it as Roark instructed.

"Make sure you check in with me regularly."

The scout nodded as she again vanished into the darkness of the forest night. Something made Roark more nervous than usual, and it wasn't the mushrooms.

~~~

The night passed without incident, but Roark had spent its entirety feeling as if the noose were closing on her neck. She knew that those following them were aided in some way from within but had no real proof. She also knew that they didn't have to try hard to catch them when someone was providing them with directions. It was because of this realization that she made her most recent tough decision as the morning sun chased a late-forming fog away from the valley in which they rested.

The last cycle of guards was resting as the first watch prepared a cold meal. She had them restricted to minimal fires. With all of their advantages, her enemy needed no more help from within.

Roark glanced over the entire group. The women were now part of the band. They no longer appeared to be the guarded, they looked just like their guards. She was very impressed. She had never expected them to be so capable at fulfilling their roles. She hoped it was enough. A chill ran up her back to warn her about over confidence. She took the warning and walked away from the group to get her mind settled for the day and the dangerous decision she had made.

Again, the faintest hint of someone watching her trickled across her spine just before Reva was standing next to her. She could not hide the transition from her normal, harshly neutral grimace to a gentle smile of appreciation. Even though the girl was not her pupil, she beamed at her for a moment like a proud master would an apprentice who was demonstrating everything with precision.

"You were right," the girl whispered. "Someone is giving us up." She handed over a small rock that, on first impression, looked no different than any other rock that might be found discarded along the valley floor or anywhere else along the Dragon's Spine. Roark had heard of the use of similar devices to pass messages in the passes but had never seen anyone go to such an effort to disguise their deception. It wasn't usually required, and it indicated a cost and sophistication she had not expected.

"When Caleb left the camp to relieve himself, he went farther than required and toward our follower's camp. When he was sure he had not been followed, he withdrew that and dropped it."

"You are sure he dropped this? It is small and you could not have been that close in the dark."

Reva's frown barely preceded her answer.

"I was close enough to him to be splashed. When he dropped it, my hand was upon it before he had stepped completely over it. It is that stone. It was still warm to the touch from being hidden in his pants. Do you need further details? I can give them."

Roark waved any more detail away and nodded at the identification of their spy. The information was damning. That would have to be dealt with immediately.

She looked closely at the rock until she found the well-hidden pry point. It was disguised as a natural indentation in the rock and anyone who had any reason to pick it up would likely have never realized it was a container for passing messages unless they were looking for it.

That same warning shiver crawled up her back again and solidified her decision. It also warned her to keep that decision a secret a little longer, but her focus and concern seemed to have alarmed Reva. She was staring at her with a concerned look.

"It's nothing to worry about right now," she whispered and brushed a rebellious red lock away from the girl's face.

Reva threw her small frame against Roark and wrapped herself around her torso. The warrior could not feel her through the tough hide armor, but she did feel the bite of the fear that caused the scout to react in such a visible way.

She gently clutched the back of Reva's head and embraced her for a moment to forestall the panic that permeated the air.

"Shhh. Don't fret my little fox, Reva. I've seen others through worse," she lied. "We're fine. Keep up the vigil with me and we will see this through."

"I know you lie."

Roark smiled at her cunning.

"Yes, but it does you little good to share in my worries. Let me carry them for a while."

"I happen to know those shoulders are not nearly as strong and broad as they appear."

"And that is a secret we must keep from ever being known."

"Perhaps. Tell me what you need from me."

Roark considered the danger of sharing her plan with anyone. She didn't usually have a confidant and was not used to sharing even with her First. He often knew what she was thinking, so it was not really required. Again, she decided quickly.

"Head west then. Create as much sign as you can. Give me a report of our pursuers as you can and before the sun sets if you are able. I'll be casually turning us south. I need for you to try and throw them off our trail."

Reva pushed away from her a little and looked into the Guardian's eyes. The little one knew what South meant.

"I know. Go carefully and tell me of anything. I don't fear the natural inhabitants."

"But, what of our rendezvous with the caravan?"

Roark answered with a simple shake of her head.

Reva nodded. She was not a native of the south reaches of the Spine, but it was common knowledge that there were portions of the Spine that no one entered if they wished to leave. The southern reaches of the Spine did not invite visitors. It was the realm of magic and magical creatures.

"Don't let this wrinkle your forehead so." Roark brushed her thumb across the wrinkles that formed across the bridge of her nose. "I tell you, the tales are far worse than what really lies to the south. I don't go there without careful consideration. I need the help of those rumors more than I fear them."

Reva nodded, but Roark knew she was not convinced.

What Roark feared did not lie to the south. She looked down at the message stone in her palm behind Reva's back as she pulled her close again for a final embrace before letting her go. The quality of everything that had been thrown at them so far spoke of funding Roark had never seen spent in the Spine. At least it was not warded. Wards would indicate a level of investment she would probably not survive. Wizards were nothing to scoff at, and that was the only thing that had not been thrown at them so far.

Reva clutched her left hand gently as she walked away into the undergrowth. The gentle squeeze was accompanied with a promising smile. Roark felt the warm reminder of her again and the weight of her load seemed lighter if only for the moment.

As she wandered back to the camp, she pulled a small metal bar with a flat prying blade on it's end from her belt. The whole bar fit in her hand and the blade just fit into the pry point in the rock. With a constant pressure that she varied on either side of the pry point she opened the stone. The quality of the mason's work further amazed her when she saw how the well was sculpted for the rolled message.

She removed the message and pocketed the stone for her own use later. She knew better than to discard quality tools unless she had no other choice and her personal rig was designed to keep that arsenal of tools close. The thin paper was high quality as well. It was probably provided to Caleb directly by whomever paid him to report on the movements of the caravan. The meant Caleb could provide information. Roark considered that option and discarded it. The value of taking care of this immediately outweighed any gain of information in this instance.

This whole pursuit had been planned so far in advance that Roark felt a sudden doubt that she would be able to overcome what was closing in around them. Someone wanted the Princess dead and had spent a lot of leaf to make it happen.

For a moment, while she unrolled the message, she shivered to let the fear run its course. With a final shudder, she looked down at the roll.

It was two lines written onto the narrow slip of paper in a tight block of letters. The letters were written in a continuous line, without breaks of any sort, and they formed no words Roark could make out. It was a code. Sophistication, on top of expense, supported by quality material. This was no brigand band that lived in the Spine. Any doubt that lingered about that was lost.

Roark fought off the desire to rip the message into small pieces. Instead she folded it carefully. Although she couldn't read it, that didn't mean she wouldn't need it some day. Once it was folded neatly, she slipped it into the pouch with the rock.

With effort and controlled movements, she forced herself to calm her fear. She inhaled a deep breath and exhaled slowly. There was no value to the panic that washed against her mind. Inhaling again, she reached across her body to draw the stiff, thin dagger that she favored for bar fights.

The diamond shaped, finely polished blade felt very comforting as the leather wrapped handle filled her fist. Calm settled into her chest as she grabbed the blade in her left hand in a low block. Her intent flowed along her arm and she felt the blade respond in her grip. The tip that narrowed on both sides was sharpened to a needle that had pierced more than one heart or head.

She dropped the killer to her side and held it point down next to her leg where no one could see it unless they were looking at her from the side. Her steps were each measured but natural as she felt every step embolden her.

As she cleared the foliage at the edge of their camp clearing, she adjusted her face to hide any sign of her intent and found Caleb with her eyes. He was rolling up sleeping gear and preparing for them to get moving. Roark adjusted her approach to keep his back to her.

No one paid her any mind until she was directly behind her target. Noise around the camp died instantly, and she knew she had only one chance. Soon, their attention would warn him, and she would lose the initiative.

Her target stood up from his pack as his instinct for danger finally warned him he was about to die. His hand was moving from his gear to his own weapon.

Her own weapon started the attack as both hands moved at once. She reached her left arm up and around to provide force to her stab. As her hand pulled his now resisting head toward her, her right hand shoved the blade of the dagger up and forward through his spine and into his brain.

He twitched in her grasp and his attempt to defend ended. He was already dead and collapsing as she withdrew the blade letting the blood flow from the pierced brain. Her retreating step allowed the falling body to sprawl into the trampled leaves and dirt where they had camped. With no real malice, she wiped her blade on his tunic and sheathed it.

The whole scene took seconds. No one moved. Everyone stared at the Guardian leader, waiting for the required explanation.

"Search his gear. Bring me any paper, quill, ink, and message stones you find. Anything that is written." She pointed at Wade. He was Caleb's likely second. He would want to make sure Roark had reason. Roark could see the anger in his eyes, but she could also see understanding. Wade knew something, or at least had a doubt.

"If you wish to challenge me, find what I asked for or the absence of it."

It wasn't uncommon for Guardians to learn how to read. It was a common way to help children find a way out of the Spine. Caleb was a surprise to her. He had never let that ability be known and had avoided showing any sign of knowing either reading or writing. Roark shook her head at how much time it had taken to set this up. She would have to reconsider how many other Guardians were hiding secret alliances. As quickly as the thought flitted across her mind, a laugh filled her chest. All of them likely kept something secret, just like she did.

She turned from the body and walked toward the cold breakfast.

The Princess and her charges stared at her. She shrugged off the incident and allowed the justice of the passes to take place. The men closest to Caleb began the search and before Roark had finished breakfast they had found all of the items she knew they would. It was not a damning condemnation for a man to have pen and ink in his gear, but to have message stones proved he was providing secret communications to someone. Again, it was not enough without the eye-witness of their scout and the matching materials Roark held in her pouch. But then, in their hands, there was a bone she had not expected. She held any reaction.

As the Guardians handed over what they found, Roark pulled the matching stone and scroll of paper from her pouch calmly and held them out in her hand.

"Compare them." She patiently made sure every step was observed.

Wade took the items from Roark and looked at what they found. They were careful to compare each item. Roark knew that she was in danger. If she had killed him without just cause, then Wade could challenge her, but she was not concerned. She had the facts in her favor.

Wade found the paper, compared the quality, and pulled the message out. He unfolded it and found the matching tear that Caleb had made when he wrote the message. Any doubt that Roark was right died with that realization.

"You know what this means?"

"Yeah," Wade mumbled. "He was bought."

Roark nodded.

"Did you find the leaf too?"

Wade nodded.

"Split it among yourselves. His betrayal should pay those he betrayed."

Roark made sure her voice could be heard.

"This man betrayed you all. We are being followed because he was telling them where we were heading. He probably told them all of our plans. Leave the traitor where he lies. Let his allies deal with his body how they wish when they catch up. They are his band and brothers, not we."

Roark didn't have to tell them that anyone else betraying them would face a similar fate. That was known by them all. She closed her hand around the evidence and dismissed them to finish their prep to leave. She fingered the bone tube and pulled it out of the rest.

It was a thin length of polished animal bone. It was lacquered to protect it from moisture and each end was corked. Wax coated each of the corks. She quietly pocketed the tube into one of her pouches. What it told her would have to wait.

"Can I see the message?" the Princess asked as she walked over. The look on her face was one of sentiment.

Roark pulled it from the clutter of evidence and handed it to her.

"It's coded. I don't have time to check him for his code book or tool," she lied.

"I know, we have to move, soon."

"When they don't find his message, they will try to catch up."

She only nodded in agreement.

"When they find him…"

Her nod became more emphatic.

With a hand motion, the Princess called over Alexa and handed her the message. It required no conversation. Alexa unfolded the strip as she walked back to join Elsa.

Roark slipped the tube into a pouch then took the quill, ink, and paper and sat down against a tree while they broke camp. She tore a similar strip of paper off of the same sheet and wrote a message. When it was done, she rolled it up, and slipped it into the message stone.

When everyone was ready to move, she checked their morale with a glance. Everyone was disturbed by Caleb's death, but the men understood. They showed the resolve to continue. The women showed the same resolve, in fact more than before. Somehow, this had energized them. Roark nodded at the result. They were not defeated.

Reva walked across the clearing to Roark. The Princess smiled at her showing both of them that she understood the girl was the reason they knew of the spy. Reva gave her a polite bow and then turned to Roark.

"Looks clear. I'll leave you a sign."

"Good. Check back in when we set up camp or when I need to know something. We will be moving slow. I need to throw them off as best as we can. If you observe them finding the body, I'd like to know how they react."

Reva nodded and looked around. It was the first time she had seen Caleb's body. Roark watched her to measure how she reacted. She showed no sign either way.

Roark bent closer to her and whispered into her ear so that only she could hear, "If we become separated, for any reason, head directly south one day. It will be hard to cross the ridge, but don't avoid it. Go straight over it. On that side, find the cottage by the only stream in that vale. There is a woman there. Tell her that I sent you. She will help you find a way out. She is not nice and will not be happy to see you, she likes to be left alone. If I can, I'll meet you there in two days. If I can't, go on without us, and never come back."

Roark could feel the resistance to her instructions start in the girl's shoulders. She was going to argue.

"Don't Reva. This is the only way I can save anything from this if we are cut off. If I fail, I can save you. I must try to save you if I can't save everyone. Give me this gift. Promise me you will do that if we get separated."

She nodded her ginger head. The rebellious curl dipped from her bangs. Roark wanted to fix it, but left it.

"I have to hear your oath."

Reva turned her head to Roark's ear, and even with the cracking in her quiet whisper, Roark knew she would not fail this promise. "I swear, my love."

Without looking at each other again, they separated.

"Let's move. I'm point. Follow closely."

Roark walked across to Caleb's body and dropped the stone on his chest. The line of blood from her dagger pointed at it where it lay. Satisfied, she turned to continue the same direction they had been following when they had stopped.

"Jarvi," Roark called back over her shoulder. "Make sure we clear our track. They're sure to follow us closer now. I want to lose them if we can."

~ ~ ~

The night was quiet and deceptive. They had turned south, slowly covering their trail and leaving fake sign to draw off their pursuers. Roark was nervous about the effect this was having, and Reva had not checked in since mid day. Her last report had been about the violent reaction to the dead spy and Roark's message. She had hoped for emotion, but what Reva had reported was more than she had expected.

A cold mist was settling in among the ferns, and, even with the stimulation of the mushroom, Roark was feeling drowsy. She had been using it too long. She would have to rest soon. Three days was the longest she had ever been able to go without rest with its help and the recovery had been brutal. But this was different. It was more like something was intensifying the weight of the night.

Since she had first seen that cursed carriage nothing had been easy, but she couldn't avoid the feeling that magic was at the root of this. There was no way they could be tracking them this well in the southern reaches—some called it the Dragon's Bowels— with all they had done to thwart them.

Roark found her hand rubbing the polished surface of the bone tube. Its quality and purpose told her who likely owned it. Since she had seen it among Caleb's things, she had suspected something more than the average band of brigands was behind this. The final piece was on the board. A wizard followed them.

Roark cursed any wizard who was playing with the fabric of nature and one specific wizard as she shook her head again to clear it. The only positive in all of this was Reva. Roark gripped her dagger's hilt to avoid thinking about where the young girl might be. Maybe she was leading them off, but she couldn't be sure. She rubbed her hand over her face. The Guardian was beginning to distrust her skills of observation.

She shook her hands and kicked her feet around to get her circulation moving again. Something was wrong. She should be moving faster. She wrapped her arms around herself and suddenly her mind screamed at her. She was not cold. The night was always cooler, but she didn't feel the chill even though a fog was forming.

Panic ripped at her mind. That created around it a pocket of clarity. She was moving slower than she should be. She was not thinking clearly.

In a burst of energy she knew she would pay for later, she moved toward the Princess' guarded area in their camp. She tripped over a stump and sprawled into the loose leaves and sticks of the forest cover. Roark raised her nearly useless hands to protect herself from the fall. Discarded twigs, long dead leaves, and black, rich topsoil sprayed away from the impact which she knew had probably scraped her arms, but she didn't feel it. She was addled, and that was not good. It was as if the earth was pulling her in, and she did want to rest.

Where was Reva? Where were the others? Where were her men? She rolled into a ball and forced herself to stand even though she just wanted to lay there. When she regained her feet, she drew a small dart from her belt and drove the point into the fat of her thigh trying to avoid muscle. The tip pierced her flesh and the pain momentarily ripped the fog away. It helped clear her mind, but it was not enough. She was in some cursed wizard's spell, and the only cure for that was a dagger in his spine.

Remembering her herbs, she felt for her pouch, but her hands seemed twice as large as they should. She could not get her fingers into the pouch. She tried again, and failed. She let the panic win for a moment. She needed any boost she could get.

"Reva!" she shouted trying to use sound to break the spell's grip, but even that seemed to expand from her slowly and have no affect against the resistance. The fog seemed to absorb even sound. Her whole world was trapped in a grey tar.

"Elsa," she nearly whispered as her hands dropped to her side and she fell to her knees.

Her eyes wanted to close. The fog was closing in on her mind. The forest around her was mostly invisible in its grasp. Was it really a fog? Was it just the effects of a spell? Again she cursed all magic users. They were the foul dregs of an already foul place. She allowed her mind and her anger to think another wasted thought on how she would slowly drive a thin dagger into a defenseless wizard.

Not willing to surrender, she propelled herself on her hands and knees toward the Princess. She might still be able to save this. If she was quick. If she was lucky. If she could keep her mind from surrendering. If she could find some help. She finally heaved herself up onto her feet again.

Roark stumbled awkwardly, this time careful to watch for stumps and trees, toward where the others should be. With each step she called a name, any name. It didn't matter. She knew it. The spell had probably already subdued everyone else. She and Reva were the only ones who may have been protected with the help of the mushrooms. She hoped the little fox was not in this trap. A few more steps and she was at the pallets where the women were nested with the Princess.

Elsa was stretched out of her bedding trying to cover the Princess with her body but had only made it to her legs. Her body held the princess where she lay. Alexa was leaned up against a nearby tree. She was not moving either. A dagger, tip in the dirt, hung in her limp hand resting on her thigh.

Roark knew that she was running out of time. Her lips felt thick and heavy. Her cheeks felt like they were running off of her face like a thick porridge. She had no choice. She had to get them out of range of the wizard's spell. She had no idea how far that might be. It had to be an area spell. It would take too many wizards to do a focused spell on each of them. The struggle to get to the women had cleared the fog somewhat, but it was still not freedom. She had to get out. She had to take them with her.

"Jarvi!" she shouted vainly for help. Hoping that he would be there. Some of her men knew about the herbs she used. Maybe she would be lucky. No responses came back through the fog. She thought she shook her head in frustration, but she couldn't trust what she thought anymore.

Roark bumbled over to the Princess. When she got there, she sat beside her. Even as she settled there, she realized it was a mistake. The fatigue and fog wrapped her up as she contacted the earth. Fear screamed at her. She thought she lashed out at the fog. She had to get the Princess away. With fumbling hands, she dragged the covers of her bedding away.

The spell was earth magic, her mind told her as it caught up. It was seeping up from the ground. The fog was helping but it got stronger the more she touched the ground. She had to get up.

She thrust her hand into the dirt to push herself up, and it felt like her hand sunk in up to her elbow. The very ground was trying to envelop her. Every push felt like it was sinking into a wet mass instead of helping her stand. She managed to get a knee up and felt the drain fall off some, but she was still not clear. She pushed against the ground with her free leg and her trapped arm. Her second knee finally pulled free from the grappling ground. Triumphantly, she used the muscles in her back and stomach to jerk her hand away from the entrapping earth. She was standing again, though precariously.

With her mostly useless hands she grabbed the princess' harness. Luckily, she was still dressed in her male garb except for the outer armor. The leather strapping required to keep the armor in place created handles that Roark could use. She dragged her—unceremoniously— out of the bedding. It was a slow process. She was not sure she was making any progress at all. She had no idea how far she had to go. She didn't know where the wizard was focusing the magic. She just had to guess. Based on Reva's report about their being followed, Roark felt confident that heading away from their back path was best, but she wasn't even sure which way that was. She could only trust her instinct. She dragged the Princess deeper into the woods toward what she thought was south. Several times she collided with trees as she walked backward away from their camp. With each collision she took a moment to resettle and then moved on.

She was abandoning the others. She couldn't do any more. If she stayed, the wizard would have them both. The princess was the target. The others were already lost. Roark hated herself for that decision. If she could clear her mind. If she could get away. Then she would go back. She swore at that moment that she would return for them when she could. All she could do, as the fog held on and the ground tried to swallow her, was keep going.

The first indication that she was clear of the spell's range came in her mind. The numbness around her eyes broke and she could think more clearly. It was such a sharp difference that it seemed to smack her in the face. The mist was real, although it was probably an artifact of the spell, and it choked the forest as she tried to focus and look for a direction again. In the distance, behind them, she could see globes of light in the dark mist. Someone was moving around in the middle of the spell's area of effect. The evil globes danced around what she had to imagine was the campsite. She watched them dance as her mind cleared and she could understand what she was watching. Each globe was an enemy soldier doing what they willed in her camp. Her mind could not connect with the sounds and make sense of what was happening, but she knew it was not good. She would not be able to go back. Not now. Not until she could stand against them. Roark looked down at the still unresponsive body of the princess. She had saved her, and only her.

She had kept them from their prize, but only if she could continue the escape. She was still not clear though. Feeling was returning to her hands. She had wrapped the harness around her fingers and now they were screaming at her in pain. She relaxed her grip a little and shook them out one at a time. She didn't allow herself to let go of the Princess. She didn't want to lose her after all of that. The ground had stopped trying to grab her. She had to get away.

She immediately reached into her pouch when she could feel her fingers again and pulled out a couple more doses of the mushroom. She stuck the pinch in her own mouth first to relieve the lethargy that still haunted her. She wasn't sure how doubling the dose would affect her, but she had to take the chance. Then she took out another pinch and, pressing her middle finger between the Princess' slightly parted lips, inserted the chopped mass against the moist wall of her cheek. Any help would be better than her current state.

With the medication delivered, Roark grabbed the front of the Princess' harness and shirt and lifted her up and over her shoulder. The fungus was helping to clear the torpor, but she still stumbled under the sudden weight. She could feel her own feet again, and movement in the forest was getting easier even though the fog continued to obscure any real idea of where she was going. All she knew was that she was getting away, and the people pursuing them had a wizard working with them. That made her mission even harder, but she still had her charge.

Every contract clearly stated that any delivery guarantee was void against magic. It was clearly stated. They had to sign it. Roark laughed at the silly thoughts that filled her mind as they escaped the trap. Then her mind turned a direction she never expected. She thought about the young scout out in the fog alone. Maybe Reva got away. Maybe she would see the scarlet haired vixen again. Maybe she remembered her instructions and went to the safety ahead of them. Maybe she was already there. Her heart hiccuped at the thought of losing her after she had just found her. She was going back. If Reva was back there, she was going back with a fervor and vengeance that poor wizard never expected. In her mind she sharpened the point of her dagger against the crooked thigh bone of a wizard.

GUARDIAN'S RETREAT

Roark had stopped running as soon as the sun was up and the risk of being seen increased. The fog was behind her. She could not take a chance of being caught now, but she didn't dare stop either. The Princess was slowly recovering, but the magic's effect was powerful, and she didn't dare dose her any more. Slowly and quietly would have to do, or as slow and quiet as she could be while carrying the Princess. Safety was ahead, she hoped.

The attackers— they had stopped being pursuers when they assaulted her camp— knew more than she thought. All of her attempts to hide the princess seemed useless. They were not going to make it back to the caravan, but she had given up on that a day ago. Malich would carry on without her. He knew what she expected. She would deal with that on the other side of the Spine, if she ever saw it.

A wizard had joined the chase. No matter how she tried to shake him from her trail, he persisted. Even after killing his spy among them she couldn't lose him! Instead, he had struck. Maybe he struck because they had taken his eyes. More likely he struck because Roark had tweaked his manhood in her little message. She couldn't avoid the smile that came to her when she thought of having that effect on her attacker. It meant he was human. It meant she could kill him.

Roark struggled to keep her thoughts clear as she trudged forward with her burden. She had delayed sleep too long. No matter what she tried, sleep was going to take her. The herbs would only hold it off so long. She had run without any real rest for three days and had used it to protect her from the wizard's spell. She was on borrowed time already.

To fight off the fatigue, she forced herself to think about her problem even though she could barely focus. Attacking as soon as they did simply because she had insulted them didn't make sense. It didn't make sense for the loss of one man. The same wizard couldn't be scrying them while controlling the fog that had knocked them all out. He would need a spy to keep following them as well as they had or a tracker that was using something to help them. She never knew wizards to travel in packs, so it was unlikely that he had magical help, but somehow he was still tracking them. But that didn't explain the attack when they had such an advantage. He could have waited and followed until he could guarantee that none would escape.

She stopped to give her mind the focus it needed to consider that question. Concentration was getting harder. She had turned south. That was her last move after taking his spy. What about those two steps had caused him to act?

Roark knew the Spine would help her if she headed south into the harsher realms known as the Dragon's Bowels. It was more dangerous for her, but even worse for anyone unfamiliar with the Spine. But was it so dangerous for a wizard?

Did that scare them? Was the attack meant to keep them from reaching the Bowels? Roark nodded to the sun dappled shadows that followed her. They were afraid of the Bowels, but why? She considered the facts again to make sure she was not making assumptions.

The field against them had grown with every day they had traveled. Maybe the wizard was the last piece for which they waited. No, that still didn't explain the overkill of that attack. It exposed their power, unless they had more in reserve. That thought made Roark's weakened mind scream. She was going to have to rest soon. She hoped their attack was a response to the threat. If it was, then the wizard was concerned about something specific. Again Roark nodded to herself.

Then she smiled. It was all academic. It was a matter of pride for her now. She was alone against them, however many there were. She could only rely on herself. She couldn't trust anyone else. They seemed to have their fingers in every pocket of the Spine, but she was going to defeat them. As soon as she could rest, she was going back for the others.

A bolt of fear suddenly shook Roark's resolve. If they were in control of the Spine, like it seemed, did they have *her*?

Roark grinned confidently as she realized that must be why they attacked. They must be afraid of *her*. Roark knew she was dragging them south, but until that very moment she had not realized where she was headed. Where she had been headed since she told Reva to go there. If their attackers were still able to track them—and that seemed apparent— they would be able to predict where she was heading. If they had turned *her* then they were truly powerful, but then they wouldn't have attacked. So, they were afraid of *her*.

They had attacked to avoid being drug into *her* valley. They had limits then. Roark was not going to let them take the Princess. She would drag them into the Dragon's Bowels even if she had to drag them with their claws buried in her flesh. Then, she could escape. The she could kill them.

She had been there before, once, and she would go there again gladly to shake these demons from her tail, even if it meant her own life in the trade. All she had left of her reputation was hanging across her shoulder. But, now, more than her reputation was at stake. She forced herself to trudge onward even as the effort to think had taken her closer to the end of her reserves.

As she renewed her march, she looked around again with the hope of seeing Reva step out of the shadows. The mere thought of the petite scout caused Roark's heart to ache. If they had caught her. If they had hurt her, she would not be responsible for how she would react. Roark forced herself to calm down. The added stress of worry would deplete the meager reserves she was running on. It had been a long time since Reva had appeared. To have found someone who made her feel loved, suddenly as she had, and then to lose her in that fog, too that wizard… Roark bit off that stream before it pushed her to anger again. She could not go back after her now, and Reva had the instructions on where to go if they were separated. Roark had to continue to believe that she was safe until there was evidence that she wasn't. There was no other way she could continue.

She adjusted the Princess on her shoulder and pushed up the ridge she had been climbing.

Some time after the sun had kissed the floor of the valley below her, she realized she was finally near her relief even as her energy ebbed at its nadir. She stood on the other side of the crest of the ridge she had been climbing all morning. Below her was the familiar valley she had visited so long ago. It looked as bleak as it had so many years ago. In the very center of the valley's floor a seemingly peaceful oasis of green among the stark grey limbs cried to her to rush to it for comfort and rest. She smiled at it and wished for its promised peace. The sun flickered off of a beautiful stream in the very center of a green sward surrounded by vivid green trees casting soft shadows on the bed of grass. It seemed so out of place in the otherwise dreary valley, and yet it promised the very peace and safety that she needed. It whispered to her that her tired body needed rest. It promised to refresh her, as it had before. It was a familiar friend. It wanted to comfort her. Her steps faltered as she slowed her approach and resisted what it promised.

That last time she had been running like a flushed hare ahead of her pursuers. The inviting scene, and the promise of suffering that came if they caught her, had conspired to convince her. Her heart had pounded at her panicked mind. In her head she could not help but believe that whoever lived in such a beautiful place would help her.

She grinned at the similarity of it all. *She* would not grin. *She* would snarl, pointing at her as she shook her head. This was exactly what *she* had told her would happen. Roark had sworn it would never be true. She had sworn she would change her life and would never be at the mercy of a band of lusty men again. *She* had simply laughed.

Roark put the Princess down to take another rest that might help her resist the trap. Not far away, but not in that beautiful mirage, was a woman Roark had sworn she would never visit again. Perhaps *she* had known this would happen. Perhaps there was no way to avoid it, like *she* said.

Roark inhaled a refreshing breath to brace herself for the meeting that would come as soon as they reached the bottom of the valley. She could see the light flickering off of the brook that attracted them all, just like it had attracted her the first time.

It would not be a pleasant reunion if she made it. Her energy was flagging. She could feel the deferred sleep pulling at her like a quagmire. She would not be able to avoid it much longer.

Without thinking she reached for the Princess to throw her over her shoulder again, and what had been an unconscious form shifted away from her. Roark had not even noticed that she was awake. Relief allowed her to surrender more to the fatigue that was beating at her.

"I am capable of walking on my own now," Cinnia said proudly. "But, It would be good of you if you would tell me where we are, and where the others are as well."

Roark stumbled a little at the change as she fought to maintain her upright attitude. Realizing she was shutting down, Roark flattened the palm of her right hand and struck herself roughly across the right cheek. The makeup did nothing to hide the bright red hand print that exploded onto her face. It was not as hard as someone else would strike her, but it was enough to stave off the fatigue she was losing to.

Cinnia leaned away from the violent demonstration and stared at Roark.

"I've been— putting off, mmmmh, sleep with Night Warden,... dried mushroom that stimulates. I used it to wake you from— sleep you were in." She was not sure, but she thought she might be slurring her words.

"Then, we were attacked last night?"

"Yeah," Roark groped for more words.

"The others?"

Roark could see the worry on Cinnia's face, but for some reason she could not avoid laughing. She bit it off with effort when her face hardened at the Princess' state. With improved control, she answered.

"Captured... or killed," she slurred.

"Even Reva?"

"Not... Not sure."

That seemed to make the Princess smile. Roark smiled too and started to sit down. Instead she toppled to the floor of the forest.

"I think you should stand. Maybe you should lean on me."

"We need to... get down the..." She pointed down toward the valley floor and rolled over onto her knees. "No... Not there." She pointed down stream from the glamor. She could barely focus on what she knew was not real and point out the shack down stream where they would find *her*.

"Probably sooner than later," Cinnia commented as she caught Roark's arm and slung it over her shoulder to help her stand. Roark looked at her with very wide eyes and little understanding.

"Are you sure that is safe?"

"No," she giggled, "it's not s…safe. But it is where we must go. *She* knows I'm coming."

Cinnia nodded and pulled her toward the shack.

They walked down the most accessible defiles for a way. Cinnia helped guide Roark across the rocks as quickly as they could move. Roark stayed awake but only enough to mumble directions and point at what she remembered. She knew *she* would find them when they were close. *She* never let strangers wander her valley. *She* would soon close the net around them.

"I… sorry I let you down." Roark mumbled at some point as they struggled across a difficult pass.

"On the contrary," Cinnia said calmly as she held Roark up and pointed at a series of step like rocks. "You have most assuredly saved me again."

Roark's vision was starting to fade more. It was becoming darker and darker even though she knew it was midday.

"Have we lost… the… the day already?" She asked looking up with her head wobbling about and nearly toppled them both.

"No, it is still day. I'm afraid you are not going to get much farther without me carrying you."

Roark laughed without thinking. It was absurd to think that the Princess could carry her. She was but a waif in this wilderness. Roark's body tingled and the princess exhaled as if a weight had settled upon her. Roark continued to giggle as she dropped to her knees in the rough wash they were navigating. She looked about herself as she felt the last of her energy bleed away. Hands, someone's hands, wrapped around her chest as she fell forward and lowered her gently to the rocks.

Roark remained on the edge of consciousness as someone, not the princess, lifted her as if she were a bundle of rushes and carried her down the wash. She could not be sure how long it took. She could not promise she had not slept for most of it.

Voices, not friendly, but also not hostile, talked occasionally.

Then, like a light through a moonless night a voice she knew spoke to her.

"So, little dove, you came back," *She* said. "I told you you would. No matter your promise, like I told you. You came back to invade my little glen."

Roark could not reply.

"Yes, and like I warned you then, it is because of your folly. You bring trouble with you as always, and, oh, what trouble it is this time. Trouble sure. Trouble enough to end us all. Titch. Titch."

~~~

Voices that were similar to what she remembered as she was carried down the ravine filtered into Roark's suddenly sensitive ears. Again, she was naked and clean. A memory of soft caresses from what seemed such a long time ago bubbled up in her memory.

The sudden thought of Reva, who Roark had not seen in what she believed was two days, caused her to sit up and open her eyes. Her heart pined for her scout to be there, sitting next to her. As quickly as her hopes leapt to the front, they were dashed by reality. No one sat waiting for her to wake. Roark slumped against her elbows in the covered rushes.

She was in a bed. The smell of rose, lavender, and cinnamon reminded her yet again of Reva. Frustrated,

Roark tossed off the coverlet and stood in the chilling morning air. Her body guessed at the time of day, but other scents told her that it was right. The voices that whispered in the other room of the cottage were amiable.

Roark's gear was stacked on a chest at the foot of the bed. She ignored it for a moment and pulled down a robe that was hanging next to the door. The linen was of good quality for the Spine. It was probably stolen from a caravan and sold through the distribution markets. Smart caravans bargained to trade items like that for passage through dangerous areas. In Roark's business it was part of the contract to provide a portion as a bargaining tithe for the whole train. Just smart business. It worked for her. Thoughts of her now far-off band also plucked at her heart. A tough day protecting a caravan would be pleasant compared to where she found herself.

Roark stuck those thoughts into a safe place in the back of her mind. Self-pity was nearly as deadly as self-doubt. It just worked more slowly.

A curtain blocked the entrance to the only other room in the cottage. Roark brushed aside the rough woven cloth that was designed more for warmth than comfort and stepped into the room.

The hearth was banked and throwing welcome heat into the room. Cinnia in all of her glamour sat at the rough-cut, square table that had seen all manner of things stain its surface. The gold-trimmed white dress she had worn that first day clung to her shoulders and hinted at the secrets the Spine wanted to harvest. Across from the dangerous beauty, sat her absolute opposite. *She* was the very example of a witch. Her skin was tinged with the unhealthy colors caused by plying the darker forms of magic. Blemishes and blights covered her exposed skin and most likely that which was not exposed. Her hair was a matted nest and a blend of all the colors ever seen in human hair. Wild strands of brilliant black and equally bright white hair shot through the mass, defying any blade to cut them or comb to tame them.

The only thing that could be considered beautiful on the woman were her eyes. Roark avoided using that exact term to describe them. The brightness they cast, joined with the obvious hate that burned like facets in the most valuable gems, melded to create a charming and terrifying gaze. Roark had heard of powerful gazes that froze people in place, and this one proved the legends.

Roark knew that the hatred in the gaze was not directed at her, but it encompassed all of humanity that *she* held in contempt.

"Well, little dove, you are alive after all. I will have to pay up on the wager I had with your prize here. I thought you were dead, just waiting for your specter to realize it. In fact, I hoped it was true. I would benefit twice from that. I needed a revenant to play havoc with, and yours in particular to help my own future. I may still get one yet, if your look and the bones I cast are to be trusted. There's a good chance your body will fertilize the fields afore the week is out."

Roark remembered how difficult it had been to talk with the witch the last time she had visited her. *She* had not changed.

"You are as hospitable as always, Dara."

The witch hissed and made a complex sign in the air at Roark's use of her name. It was the one thing Roark had learned while visiting that could not be taken back and was valuable to the witch. It vexed *her* still that Roark knew it.

"If you value your hide," *she* pointed at Cinnia, "you will forget that you heard that, either voluntarily or involuntarily." The knarled, cracked finger and blackened fingernail was as threatening as the words.

"I assure you," Cinnia's words were as melodic as Dara's were dissonant, "I have already forgotten it. I've never asked your name, and I need not know it. Your hospitality does not require familiarity."

The effects of the words were not lost on Roark. Somehow, Cinnia had found a way to mollify the hatred that oozed from Dara. She had bearded the dragon. For a moment, the hatred in her eyes even dimmed and a hidden beauty almost shimmered around her. When Dara saw Roark's look, the fire relit.

Cinnia seemed to be grinning at the effect. Roark noted it and sat down with them.

"You say hospitality. I say patience. Not long now, you'll be gone, and I'll be back at peace. Those after you will only wait so long. I scare them, but there is a threat closer that will force them to act. You'll be gone before that, you will."

"We need to press your hospitality for a few days," Roark said.

Dara again scribed an invisible mark in the air as if it would block or capture Roark's words.

"No. No. No. You go, live or dead, now!"

"I trust Roark has a reason for asking for this time from you. We can make it worth your risk." Cinnia's vocal appeal seemed to be working, then the fire in the witch's eyes flared.

"Not nice to try to manipulate me. I know your power. You cannot imagine mine, but I've known you were coming for a long time. I've known the risk since the day this little dove landed on my door trailing her first set of vile pursuers. No, the sooner you go, the less I suffer, the less I have to kill. But, I know her choices, too. She faces one she has never dreamed." The witch's crooked finger scratched at the very air between them to point at Roark with an audible scraping that made chills chase up Roark's spine.

"Can you tell us of what you have observed?" Cinnia pressed gently.

"Can I?" the witch laughed. "That's not your question. Your question is will I?"

"You are correct. I do hope that you will."

"No." With the single refusal Dara stood from her perch and walked toward the door. "There it is again. Something different teases at my borders. Something I can't see, but I know it comes. It comes again. This is unforeseen and I hate things I cannot see."

Roark stood and looked at Cinnia.

"Perhaps it is best if we get going. I have already risked too many lives by sleeping this long."

Cinnia looked up at her with a pained gaze.

"Do you think there is any chance any of the others survived at all?"

"I'm not sure, but I'm tired of running."

"No. No," Dara cried at the ceiling and rushed as fast as her humped back allowed to the hearth and the cauldron that boiled on its fire. As she approached it, she grabbed a miscellany of items scattered on a nearby shelf. When she reached the cauldron's edge, she tossed them all neatly into the steaming liquid as if she were adding spice to a stew. A flash, then smoke curled up from the surface. Dara stared into the tendrils of the steam and smoke through the crooked, crossed fingers of her hands. For a moment Roark thought she saw figures moving within it, but she could make no sense of the dancing smoky columns.

"Nooooo," Dara hissed in a pleading moan and turned to face them. Her actions had stopped all conversation.

"Head south. Yes. Go now. They will not follow, not through this valley. They will go around me. You should go south. Abandon any thoughts of going back. Pain is where you have been."

"Is that what you scried just now?" Cinnia asked sweetly as if she were a student looking for instruction. "Is that actually what you saw?"

Dara grinned up at the princess with a malicious grin of crooked, rotten teeth. Roark saw the terrifying pleasure of success play across the witch's face as she started to answer.

"Yes," she said sweetly.

"Is it?" Cinnia asked again, and Roark could feel the pressure of her question against the witch's willpower.

"No," the witch spat on the floor. Smoke climbed from where her spittle landed. Roark looked at Cinnia unsure what had just happened. The princess shook her head as if she didn't know either.

"No, what I saw was for me. You go south, now. I will stay here and make them go around, so you go south."

"I think we have worn out our hospitality here. Are you well enough to travel?" Cinnia asked Roark. Dara shook her head in disgust.

"You're like me, you are," she whispered into the smoke curling up from her lie.

"If you don't get out of the Spine— damn the gods that brought you here— there'll be another witch to bolster their lies."

Cinnia turned to face Dara and placed her hands on her hips. The Princess' chin was thrust out in defiance.

"If you've seen something of me in there, you will tell me."

"Seen? No. No. Not seen."

Roark fell back on her heels and turned toward the room where her gear lay. Those eyes that never showed anything but hate were filled with fear and it chilled the Guardian like nothing she had ever seen in the Spine. Roark looked from the witch to Cinnia and back as the two women stared at each other. There was something between them that Roark had not understood, not until that moment. There was more to the Princess' story.

"You know her story because you lived it," the suddenly enlightened fighter said to the two women.

"A version of it, little dove. This one walks my path, but there's a chance for her. She has a hero I didn't have." The haggard face that had represented something to be feared for so long turned to look at Roark and almost smiled at her. "Your story is mercurial and so fun to watch in the steam and smoke of the dragon's breath. Yes. Yes. You are as much a part of the Spine as I am."

She pointed her bent and cracked finger at Roark and then at herself.

"Yes. Yes." She nodded and sighed a heavy sigh. "You and I will never escape it and for the same reason. She—" Her finger slid across the room scraping the air again as it moved. "—She has a chance because of you, but it depends on which path you chose."

The woman who had represented fear to Roark for so long seemed to shrink in front of her. Years of age slumped onto her back and bent her deeper.

"Your choice decides many things, as I saw when you first came here. I couldn't tell you then, and I can't tell you now because that would be much worse. This is bad enough. You go. You go and with you goes the very heart of the Spine. What you protect this day, hero, is another chance. A chance you never knew. A chance you will never have, but others will. You must leave now, for I must prepare for what comes. I fear it is the dragon's breath this day. Your choice. Yes. Yours."

The woman turned from both of them shaking her head back and forth as she walked across the room. She stopped as if something had blocked her and she looked down at the ground. Roark looked over to Cinnia who was standing with her left hand across her mouth. She was shaken by whatever had stopped Dara. Roark could feel within herself the very reverberations of what had happened.

Roark looked around the cottage with a sense of foreboding.

"What are you saying? What comes this day? What choice did you ever give me?"

The woman shook her head. "Your decision has been made since the day you first came here. That was what I hadn't realized. I should have known then. Your choice was never in doubt. You made it then. You'll never visit me again, little dove. No. This is our end. It is."

She turned around finally and looked directly into Roark's eyes from where she stood. She cocked her head at her and looked through her as if there was something inside her. A tear rolled down the witch's cheek and splashed onto the dirt floor.

"You've never understood your power little one. You've never understood what makes you what you are. Ah, but you will. Beyond this day, you will."

Dara stood up straighter than she ever had. Her hump vanished as she walked across the room in slow steps toward them. Roark wanted to run, but she held her ground. The hand that had been cracked and bent, smoothed out before her eyes as it pointed toward her chest and seemed to float up at her.

Roark heard Cinnia's intake of breath synchronized with her own.

In another step, the bent woman stood as straight and as tall as both of them.

Her ragged cloak and tangled nest of hair shifted to long golden threads and a silvery tunic that fell across curves as beautiful as Roark had ever seen.

The skin, darkened by magic and age, smoothed and glowed in the light of the fire. Every blemish faded away before their eyes as the finger stabbed her in the chest. It felt almost as if the woman had thrust a dagger into her heart. Roark looked down to make sure she was not killed, but the finger simply pinned the robe to her chest.

"In here." She tapped Roark's chest. "The Heart of the Dragon beats. I knew it the first day I saw you. They chased you because you stood up to them, but it was more than just that. They chased you because you chose to defend someone. Someone who reminded you of your sister. Someone you wouldn't watch them destroy, but they chased you because you represented a shift in power."

A tear broke away from Roark's eye and rolled onto her cheek.

"That was what I saw come running into my valley. You, little dove, stood up to the lot of them. You killed one of them before they knew you were upon them. Another had fallen in the chase. You were just learning what you could do."

The now tall and slender woman who had been a haggard old witch turned to look at Cinnia.

"This is the child that ran directly to me, bringing those beasts with her. She had nothing left in her and collapsed in the glen to rest and drink. I barely stopped the magic from killing the poor child that day for she was naive."

Dara's soft hand caressed Roark's cheek lovingly, like the mother Roark had barely known.

"And from that day I knew, as well as I know now, that she would change things. I am legend beyond the Dragon's Spine, but she will be so much more. She will shake the entire land. But the cost will be dear, for she will awaken opposition that has slept. When she stands up, it will be far worse than what I have done. It will be far worse than any of us have done."

She again looked at Roark. The eyes were the same, but the hate was replaced by something else.

"That is why I told you nothing then. That is why I don't want you to do the very thing that your heart requires of you. The very thing that drove you here, brought you back as I knew it would."

The eyes showed sadness.

"You will make the decision I have always known you would. What I realized today is that you had already made the decision before you came here back then. We were destined to this path even though the fates continued to believe there were alternatives. I'm not sad for me— the end was always at hand— but I'm sad for the yoke you take up. You don't even realize its weight, and yet you take it."

Dara's pattern of speech had changed, but Roark still didn't understand what she meant. She turned to Cinnia.

"You see it?"

Cinnia nodded. "Yes."

"Her innocence makes it tragic."

"Yes."

"I have to prepare. You will take care of her?"

"Yes." Cinnia placed her hand on Roark's shoulder.

~~~

Roark woke again as the sun crested the edges of the Spine. She was still not sure how many days had passed. The night chill had sunk into her bones and threatened to make it hard to move. She was covered with her traveling blanket, but she was still wearing her armor. She sat up, discarding the blanket to free her arms. She needed to know where she was.

Below them, the sward and stream still beckoned to her. Roark rubbed at her eyes both to free them from the dryness of sleep and to give them a chance to adjust before she looked again at what surrounded her.

Cinnia lay on a slab of stone nearby, uncovered, wearing the remains of her male attire and looking as beautiful as she ever had yet decidedly not male.

Ashes of a small fire in a ring smoldered and stank of the blend of ash and moisture that gave Roark an idea of how long it had been cold. Agitation bubbled up at the fact that there had even been a fire. After trying so hard to get them away, a fire was not wise, but given the lack of gear it was the only appropriate way for them to stay warm through the night. It did look appropriately small and well prepared. Roark nodded in appreciation of the effort by someone she had otherwise thought had limited skills. There was more beneath the surface of this princess.

The lethargy of the sleep brought on by the herbs clung to her, but she had to move. She had to assess their situation.

Her gear was sitting next to her. She clutched the belt of tools and swung it around her waist as she looked around. Lack of information made her nervous.

They were sleeping just over the crest where she had laid the Princess down to rest what seemed to her to have been a day before. Had they not made it to the valley floor? Had they not struggled down the defiles? What of that had actually happened?

Roark shook her head. What had happened? Had she really talked to Dara? She focused on determining their risk instead of the more fantastic questions. She walked up to the crest of the ridge to see if she could see anyone who had followed or found them.

Cinnia stirred from her makeshift bed as Roark was walking back. If anyone was following them, they were wisely staying hidden.

"Good Morning."

"Aye, it is good since we still live."

Roark pointed to the fire in the ring. "Your work?"

"Yes."

"Not bad for a pampered noble." She tried to smile to soften her anger over the possible exposure. "Dangerous... but not bad."

"I felt the risk was minimal, and you were not doing well at all."

"Since we are still here, it seems we have not been followed. Can you tell?"

"I've watched for sign of them. I've seen nothing approach us from any direction."

Roark chose to let it go. She was still trying to figure out what had really happened. She felt too well-rested to have slept on a rock all night. She had memories that didn't match having recovered out in the elements. However, everything said they had stopped here and rested, and for more than a day based on the signs around her.

"Then, you were my Guardian while I recovered. I owe you, and I apologize for putting you at risk. We made this valley, which was my goal and apparently without being followed."

"A debt already paid, I assure you. You seem troubled."

"A dream, I assume. A bad one."

"Would you like to share it? I've talked with no one since you dragged me to safety."

"No. I fear what telling this dream will mean. We need to pull things together and decide our next steps. We have been lucky that we were not taken while we rested here. This is not the safest place."

"I assume we continue south as we had planned and then cross the Spine to get to the Parthian border."

Roark could feel the glare form on her own face and suppressed it. Cinnia looked at her with concern.

"That was your original plan. We continue with that, correct?"

Roark could not suppress her confusion and then forced herself to believe that the dream was just that. Dara had not spoken to them.

"No. Not now. Not after they attacked us. No." She paced in the small space between their rocks. Roark could feel the anger at having to explain this to the Princess fill her and paused to calm herself.

"They took prisoners, that is the only reason to attack us. I was protecting your whole party. I can't have them holding anyone."

"And you wish to avenge this attack," Cinnia finished the unspoken thought.

Roark brushed the ground off of her trousers as if the action would stop any argument. The Princess nodded. Roark did not deny her point. She did not agree with the plan, but she also didn't question it.

Quickly, Roark took inventory of what they had. They only had the food Roark carried with her as survival rations. It was enough to keep her alive for a little while, but it would only last a day or so keeping two alive. She could not tell by looking around the camp how long they had actually rested here.

"Reva?" Roark asked the question she was more worried about.

Cinnia looked at the ground. "I have not seen her, not since before we set up camp the night they attacked."

Roark nodded. She wanted to ask how long ago that was, but she didn't feel that Cinnia knew either.

Roark pulled on the rest of her discarded gear and checked everything as she did. She had all of her weapons and personal gear, but she was alone. It was clear that the enemy had breached the honor of the

Guardians' code. There was something very powerful at work here.

Roark looked down at the cottage and glen below her, again. Had they really slept here? It didn't match how she felt. She was too rested. She looked at Cinnia again to see if there was any indication in her appearance. The woman looked like she had abandoned any hope of looking like a man other than the clothes. She was not as polished as she had been when she entered the Spine, but she also didn't look like she had before the attack. Cinnia had been the hardest to disguise. None of that told her any more than she already knew.

The princess had a question but chose not to ask it. Roark gave up the chase and returned to planning how she was going to accomplish her mission.

She settled onto a rock hidden behind low scrubs at the top of the ridge that looked back toward their old camp. Her only choice to get the princess away clean was to head southwest. She would have to maintian the ridges to protect them from their pursuers. They would track them easily in the valley, but along the ridges she had an advantage.

But she couldn't leave the others behind. Her mind immediately thought of young Reva in the hands of a wizard. They were brutal on their best day, and this time they did not get their prey. They would want to find the true object of their search.

She felt a pang of regret stab her as she thought about the young girl and her unclear fate. It was better for her if she were dead. Roark forced her thoughts back to the analysis. Reva's revelation proved that their plan had been shared. She had killed the spy and cut off the flow of information. The brigands had still found them… in spite of active attempts to throw them off the trail.

The wizard's trap was already sprung before they had stopped for the day. They were not using traditional tracking methods. The fact that a wizard was working with the brigands explained why her gut had been agitated, but even they needed focus for their magical search. The entire region of the pass was too much area for one wizard to search alone, and Roark hoped— actually quietly prayed to a long-forgotten deity— that they followed their traditional pattern and traveled alone. Somehow the wizard had reduced the large search area to a more manageable region. Without the spy providing information, how was the wizard doing it while moving? She had never heard of one scrying while moving. They had to rest and be stationary for a while.

Roark knew the track to the south would keep them hidden. She could do it without leaving any signs of their progress since there were only two of them. But, somehow, even with Reva focusing on throwing them off, they had left some trace.

"Cursed wizards. May salamanders feast on their spleens," Roark wished aloud.

The look on Cinnia's face puzzled Roark as she continued to work through what to do. It almost seemed like she wanted to defend the men who were obviously trying to kill her, but that could not be the case. She had to have misunderstood her.

"I'm going back for whoever survives and to figure out who's at the heart of this. We've run until we're nearly dead, and they're not showing sign of losing our trail. We must take an active hand in our survival."

The Princess looked to the west and then south into the valley before she looked up at Roark.

"I trust your judgement, but I will be nothing but a hinderance in your efforts."

Roark chose not to ignore the honesty of the statement. "Yes, but I think we can make you safe here for a time if you're willing."

Again, she looked around herself. Roark expected fear to be her first response, but instead she presented a regal acceptance of the necessity and simply nodded. When Roark paused to consider her reaction, it matched better than her assumed response. It also helped that she was not arguing the point.

"I'm going to see what I can find. I have to tell you that I hold very little hope. There is a chance that they think someone has information they can extract. I can make no promise of their safety, but the wizard who travels with them is looking for you, no doubt. He needs fresh information. If he thinks they hold it, they may yet survive." The thought of Reva lying among the dead in their plundered camp caused Roark to shiver. She could only hope she was safe. As it was, Roark was struggling to keep from letting her anger and frustration turn into rage and lust for revenge. She had seen how that turned out and knew she had to remain logical.

"I don't want to have to worry about you. This valley seems to keep them at bay. I'm going to use that to our advantage, but it may only be temporary. Stay alert. If you see anyone coming this way except me, you will leave immediately and head directly south across this valley. I'll either catch up with you or I'll be dead."

Cinnia nodded gravely.

Roark reached into her pouches and removed the emergency jerky and hardtack that she kept on hand. It was all that she had left. It was enough for her for a slim couple of days.

"Take this, eat what you need to keep your strength up, but you should probably save what you can. When I get back, we may not have time to slow down to hunt."

"I can't really believe you're only going back there to get the survivors," Cinnia said with probing intent.

"I have to admit, this is not all about a rescue. I want to know why there is a wizard chasing us, like I said."

"Is that all?"

"No. They're not going to give up on this search. Somehow they knew we had decoyed them with the carriage, probably because of the spy. But then they knew we were taking this particular route even though we decoyed them. I'd like to know how they knew that. If I happen to get a chance to slip a knife into a wizard's kidney and watch him twitch as he dies, so much the better for us all."

The Princess looked at her. Shock and momentary judgement in those gentle eyes hurt Roark, but she knew the Princess could never understand the brutality of the Spine and the necessity to use force to protect them.

Roark wanted to know who all had aligned with their pursuers. She was getting tired of having the Spine turn on her, a Guardian who had put her life on the line for them all. She was tired of having outsiders control everyone's lives. Roark was starting to feel that it was time to clean up things a bit. She wanted to know who she needed to kill, and she was beginning to think the list was going to be quite long. She was tired of being on the defensive and running— a losing bet based on all evidence— and that was all she had done since they had arrived at the caravan town. It was time to start fighting her way through this conflict if she hoped to live through it.

GUARDIAN UNMASKED

The Spine was a wide range of ridges created by a thrust fault. The lunging spires that pushed up out of the earth across the wide east to west band bisected the known land mass of the realms until it spread out like the wings of a dragon as it melded with the northern frozen wastes. The ridges formed a maze of passes and valleys, but all of them had a similarity. The valley walls were mostly vertical with occasional sloping approaches. This characteristic made the Spine a perfect no-man's-land where the outcast and those who preyed on them could hide and do as they pleased.

For those familiar with the geography, it was easy to pick paths that gave them the advantage over anyone foreign. That was why anyone hunting for someone in its passes and hidden vales hired a local. It was also why no realm had ever tried to invade or pacify the Spine. Cohesive armies which relied on the overwhelming force of unit maneuvers and reinforcement to defeat other armies did not fare well in the restricting confines of the Spine. That was the advantage Roark hoped to press against the men resting in the valley below her hidden overlook.

The place they had chosen was probably one of the best for them. To avoid being constantly at risk from attack from the walls surrounding them, they had selected an area where they could place guards above their base and control the approaches. It was almost like a castle carved from the stone of the Spine with a courtyard where they could encamp in the safety of their nearly vertical walls.

The problem with their choice was that their walls were porous and not nearly as vertical as they seemed. A native who knew how to navigate them could find ways to remain hidden while slipping over the crest and down into the encampment. As always in the passes, the only safety was in the hands of the men who guarded you.

It was clear that the brigand band that was harassing them was too big and unfamiliar with the Spine to know how to take total advantage of their citadel of thrusting rock. Their leader had done his best. There were guard posts above them that allowed them to look back into the camp and north and south up the ravine where they were camped. They had choke points both north and south that forced anyone coming to the camp to narrow to a two column march. But they could never control the sides where the real threat would come from. Anyone could be just over the ridge hidden by thrusting spires or slipping down on them among the defiles which cut diagonally across the walls.

Roark, sliding down a defile that hid her from the two sentries on the western ridge, was slowly improving her position over the small encampment and reading how their forces were deployed.

It was a band of slightly more than thirty men holding the valley, which most would consider overkill for the target. Anywhere outside of the Spine, Roark would have agreed. Still thirty men was quite a force for one Guardian, a pair of ladies-in-waiting, and a novice Princess, but she was not just any Guardian.

What held a force like this back? Thirty men could have taken them at any point before or after the wizard struck. They were being cautious of something. It had to be the natural lack of knowledge about the Spine, or fear of something.

Roark continued to remind herself that she was inside the enemy's borders as she dropped back below a screening cover of rock that concealed her as she watched. She hated to leave the guards at her back, but she couldn't take the time to clear them. It had already been too long and there were delicate lives at risk. She was somewhat appeased by the fact that as she drew closer to the courtyard of the pseudo castle, the archers in the "towers" would be at the outermost range for their bows.

Any time she was watching the camp below, she was somewhat exposed to the "tower" guards, set in pairs to provide the best coverage of all approaches. She knew that the northern guards could not see her because of the spire that stood between them. The southern guards were not looking. They were focused on the pass and ignoring any threat not pushing through that narrow opening that nothing would attack through, only occasionally taking a break to look anywhere else. However, the guards to the east were able to see her if they were able to overcome both the setting sun in their eyes and the shadow cast on the ridge down which she slipped.

A roaming force of guards paced a square in the floor of the valley in a very regular pattern. A single Sergeant-At-Arms checked those rovers while keeping an eye up toward the higher posts, but his pattern was the only random activity in the guard. Roark easily timed their pattern while watching the Sergeant.

She kept to the shadows as she took a chance and dropped over her screening rocks to a lower defile that took her back to the north. She had to be smart about her assault, but she could not waste time. She felt a need to move as quickly as she could without risking herself.

Half of the force was deployed defending the camp. The others did what all soldiers did when they were not on duty. They were either asleep, working on their gear to keep their readiness level high, or were engaged in any number of games of chance that maintained the balance of their income across the force. The guard had just changed to the first night watch as the sun was setting, so most of the men were settling in to sleep. A hand full remained awake.

Roark quickly identified the leaders of the force. The discipline and focus of the troops told her these were no conscripts. These were all men-at-arms who had land behind their commitment which made buying them difficult if not impossible. She didn't have time to play the slow game, but it helped her understand her enemy. This was an organized army, not a band of mercenaries. It also looked like she had intelligent leaders who knew to keep the patrols balanced so the troops were not standing post too long without a break. They were keeping them fresh and supported in teams of two, not individuals.

Roark committed the layout of the camp to memory so she would not be lost when she made it down among the tents. There were two bands of soldier pup tents lined on the east and west side of the ravine. This was an interior defense line for the three tents set up in the middle of the camp. Each tent faced the entrance of the others creating a triangular court where a common food and entertainment circle was always manned. A single guard from the next relief was tending a rock weasel over the fire. The camp was not planning on moving if the troops were able to hunt and cook their catch. Another resting soldier played a tune on a green reed pipe he had cut recently from the screening reeds that grew along the brooks that ran out of the mountains of the Spine.

The sun from over her shoulder was fading in the valley, and as it slid up the far wall it drew her attention to a colorful strip of fabric that looked out of place in the brown and metal of the guards. Laying just under the edge of the tent closest to her, a red ribbon fluttered in a light breeze. Her quest ended here if this was what she thought it was. How Alexa had kept her ribbon amazed Roark, but it was there and flapping with a pattern that didn't match the wind. She was trying to draw attention.

The fluttering fabric gave Roark hope and as quickly dashed her heart against the rocks. If Alexa's sign was all that was visible, what had happened to Reva. The scout surely would have left some kind of sign if she were able. Second, the way the fabric fluttered at the base of the tent wall seemed frantic. Roark couldn't let her emotions drive her or they would all be dead. Roark forced herself to calm by taking a drink from her water bladder. The lukewarm liquid simply kept her thirst away, but the act forced her mind to refocus. She knew where her target was. Now it was time to move.

She had navigated to the base of the western wall. The defile she was in was her best chance. It ran all the way to the bottom of the ridge and came in behind the northern-most of the tents in the triangle. She still had to navigate the band of soldiers' tents that lined this side of the camp. She had no choice, she would have to brazenly walk into the camp. Her advantage was that they had set up a latrine near the point where the valley sloped up and irregular boulders created a screen.

Roark scanned the far side of the valley one last time looking for signs that she had missed any other hidden guards. Based on the numbers resting, she had counted their balance deployed around the camp. If there were surprises out there, they were supported from somewhere other than this camp. Her eye caught another flash of red on the rocks across from her. She immediately stilled all movement and focused on where it had been while keeping her eyes relaxed to see movement around where she was looking.

It was gone as quickly as she had seen it, and she questioned if it had been nothing more than a glint of sunlight on the rock until she saw the wavering stem of a grabber thorn. The thin but wiry vines were great indicators that something was in the area. Nothing could pass near them without catching one of their tenacious barbs. Something had passed through that space.

Roark watched for other sign, but nothing appeared. There was an unknown agent out there, and she was not sure if it was an enemy or neutral. She knew she had no friends within the guarded boundary of her enemy. This increased the risk of her action, but she could not afford to delay. Her tactical decision to get into the camp without reducing her odds was designed to help the prisoners. Once she found them, she could plan how to get them out. The frantic fluttering of the ribbon told her that she had to act now to help Alexa. She would figure out what that meant as soon as she was on the other side of the line of tents. Every moment she waited increased the suffering of whoever was frantically waving that ribbon. She watched the opposite wall until the vine stopped wavering in the failing sun. Nothing else moved. It was time.

With a quick glance at all of the "tower" guards, a check on the roaming guards' position, and a final look at the Sergeant-At-Arms, she slipped from shadow to shadow until she was walking back toward the camp from the general area of the latrine she had seen others use throughout her approach. She took a casual stance, adjusted the crotch of her trousers, lifted her belt, and strode toward a tent she had marked as unoccupied. She mentally focused on walking and looking as much as she could like the other guards resting around her. There was nothing she could do to her makeup, so she focused on her presence and projected what she knew they wanted to see. At least in her mind she could be the form they would believe. A warm tingle rushed over her skin as it always seemed to when she was focusing on appearing right to her own soldiers. She felt confident that this was going to work.

A resting soldier looked up from his pallet as she approached and grunted as he shifted a rock away from his shoulder. Her heart raced as she forced herself to remain calm. She was not an invader coming to kill them all. She was an ally returning from a break.

The shifting warrior resettled. She walked on until she was standing at the unoccupied tent next to him. She toed a few items around as if she was looking for something and then continued her walk toward the center of the camp.

Forcing herself to look calm and unconcerned she again checked the "towers", roamers, and the Sergeant. None were paying her any mind now that she was inside the perimeter of tents.

The whistle of the badly tuned reed grated on her already tight nerves, but she put it aside as she walked toward the central circle of light where the fire burned. Avoiding the center, she turned before she would be clearly seen. The entrance to the southern tent where she had seen the ribbon was closed. As she approached it, she could hear the rhythmic grunting of someone inside the tent.

She had heard the noise of sex in a camp before, but this had a different sound. The brutal edge of rape seemed to fill the air, but there was something missing. She listened carefully as she continued her casual walk toward the flap. Then, beyond the grunts of activity she heard a whimpering wail of long over taxed vocal chords simply whining out for help.

She reached for the flap and a voice behind her spoke.

"Getting ahead of the line, eh."

The piper stopped brutalizing the pipe. "Rank 'as its privilege."

The sneer in the comment was evident. The shrill, untuned reed fluted at her as she forced herself to continue into the tent. With her body blocking their view and the darkness as her assistant, she drew her preferred dagger with her right hand as her left drew back the flap. She stepped in with authority.

A lantern cast an eerie light across a tableau Roark would never be able to forget.

A brute in a chainmail shirt lifted above his gyrating hips was grunting satisfactorily into a limp form covered in blood from brutal lacerations caused by the biting and cutting links and other tools that had been applied. His hands were clasped about the once living woman's throat in a brutal stranglehold that had mercifully broken her neck some time ago. The beast cared little about her. He struggled for some unreachable release and would only stop when it was met.

Roark maintained her control even though rage coursed through her. It would do her no good to draw his attention too soon, and there was nothing she could do for his victim. She allowed the flap to fall behind her before she moved. The grunting beast was lost in his oblivious search and cared not that she had entered. Watching the hulk pound himself into the flesh of a woman she had seen alive and vigorous only a day before decided for her. Sure of her footing, she drove herself across the room.

She had moved before she was sure the tent was empty. It was a dangerous mistake to make, but she was already across the room before she felt the cold surge of fear warn her there was someone else in the room. She was committed to the attack at this point. If she failed to kill the brute, she would be next on the ground. His frenzy was complete. Just before the long blade pierced his neck, his humping stopped and a questioning grunt escaped his throat as he realized she was there. He sniffed at the air with an agitated searching. With a straightening of her right arm and a bracing against the inevitable resistance, she drove the sharp point into the space just beneath the knot in the back of the brute's skull. The blade neatly severed the chord that allowed what little intelligence the beast had to send impulses to the arms and legs that still clutched at Elsa's dead form. It was overkill, but Roark allowed her extension to drive the blade all the way into the top of the man's head to ultimately scrape across the bone. She felt the blade drag across the back of the forehead.

In an instinctive gesture of protection, her left hand was coming up with a slender blade that was about half the length of her lead weapon. Her feet shifted back and around to face the other occupant of the tent as she abandoned the blade to the dead man's skull. Her left hand tracked up to threaten whoever was in the darkened corner of the tent.

A whimper from the corner told her that whoever was just out of her sight was not a threat. She dropped her guard and relaxed. There were no other threats in the tent. She sheathed her backup blade.

The lantern had been positioned so that it was spotlighting the actions on the ground. Roark could see where Elsa had been chained to the pole when the beast had started. Her broken and bloody wrists testified to the violence that had yanked her from the shackles on the pole. She turned the spotlight of the bullseye lantern around until it no longer spotlighted the death scene but cast light on the other prisoner. As the light exposed the legs and torso, Roark refused to breathe. If Reva was bound in that corner, she could not be sure how she would react.

The light climbed up the nude form until she could see the blonde strands of Alexa's hair. Finally, she adjusted the light until she could see the trembling form of the middle sister.

Alexa was bound to an outside pole. She was sitting with her legs turned to her left side. Her feet were chained together. Roark could not see her hands, but she was sure they were chained behind her back, and based on where she sat, were thrusting the ribbon beneath the tent wall hoping someone would save her. It seemed all of her energy was going into that one action. Roark felt the tension of discovery seep out of muscles she had not realized she had tensed. It was not Reva, and Roark felt a twinge of guilt at feeling relieved.

Alexa's eyes were open and unblinking. They were dry from being open too long, but the catatonic woman was unable to blink. The shock of the event had stunned her to a point where she couldn't do anything but stare, whimper, and wave her flag.

Roark looked around the tent. It was set up for this type of torture with shackles and chains hanging from each of the center poles. There was very little else in it except for the one lantern designed to give the second victim a good view of what happened to the first. They were softening her up to be questioned. Roark sensed that time was running short. Whoever was planning to extract information from her would know there was not much left to be seen. A nagging irritation burrowed into Roark's mind as she started searching for a key. She would return to that thought later when she had time to think it through.

With a quick glance around most of the tent, Roark knew there were no keys laying loose. She wouldn't have expected it, but she had to look. With her boot heel she kicked the heavy monster over and off of Elsa's corpse. A key would make this quicker and the search was worth the time. She didn't pause to take in the results of the beast's actions, but it was clear he was an effective killer. Not efficient, but very effective.

What she had hoped for was not true. The man was not the jailer. The only thing of interest was a stamped metal plate that hung on a gore covered chain around his neck. Roark repressed a shudder as she turned the chain around looking for a clasp or a way to release the chain. It was an iron chain with finger wide links and it was pinned together on the beasts neck like hunters marked their prize trackers. She pulled a small pry bar from her belt and pushed the two links that were pinned together apart. As it resisted, she let her anger drive into the bar. Her arms shivered and burned and finally the pin slid free. She stuck the chain in her belt to review later.

Her search for a key was useless. The guards who had watched her enter would become curious soon. Roark pulled at the shackles on Alexa's ankles and the woman's body started to shake in violent tremors. Her lips opened to speak. Roark released the shackles and covered Alexa's mouth quickly with her right hand. She couldn't afford for her to start screaming and she knew it was coming. The few moments of peace would have recharged her enough to enable her voice to draw attention. Roark whispered quiet consolations into the woman's ear as Alexa shuddered against Roark's chest. Time was running out, and she couldn't wrestle with a panicking woman who didn't recognize a rescue. Roark released the woman's mouth and slugged her. It was brutal treatment, but a quiet and unconscious woman was going to be easier to rescue. They had her primed to talk and she couldn't tell the difference between friend and foe anymore. In the back of Roark's mind, she wondered if Alexa would ever come back from the precipice to which they had driven her. It would take care to bring her back. Someone needed to pay for this, and Roark could feel her own skin prickling with anger. She could never save them if she lost her control, but she wanted to hurt them. She was tired of being hounded by them.

She thrust her hand into one of her pouches and pulled out a ring of key blanks and a file. The lock had a thin blade descending and a shorter blade on top of the pin of the key. She selected the matching blank and compared it to the lock. This was a tedious process, but it might keep her from losing her temper.

She focused on the meticulous investigation of the lock and the minor adjustments to the key that made the lock slowly surrender to her. She tested and adjusted. Each test told her how to trim the key a little more until it would finally force the lock. She shaved a little more metal off of the descending blade, inserted the key, and turned it against the mechanism. It turned and a reassuring click released some of her frustration. She pulled it free and applied it to all of the remaining locks. Soon she had the woman free from her torture chamber.

With care she laid her across her left shoulder. She might have to deal with the watchers. They were attentive when she entered the tent. Walking out with the prisoner over her shoulder would not go unseen. In a way, Roark wanted them to challenge her, but it would not go well for Alexa if they did. She shook her head to clear the fog of anger and get her mind back onto her goal. In and out with role camouflage. So far the men had seen her as belonging, she needed for them to continue to believe she did. She doused the lantern and let the tent settle into darkness and silence. She listened beyond the flap trying to decide when the piper and cook were probably not looking her way. Again, she focused on looking like she belonged.

She lifted the flap to allow her to step out into the dark around the tent. The fire's ring of light didn't reach her, but it didn't matter. She had to move with confidence now. To hide would give away her intent. She had to brazenly walk away as if she were doing what she had been ordered to do. She stepped away from the tent with purpose, taking two steps toward the northern tent just as the challenge she had hoped to avoid came.

~~~

"Who are you, and where are you taking that prisoner?"

The challenge was loud enough to draw the attention of the cook and piper in the central square. Roark stopped her departure and focused on looking like she belonged. Her right hand dropped to the throwing knives at her waist.

"I asked ya a quest'n."

Roark realized who had stopped her. The Seargent-At-Arms must have been crossing the clearing to check the other side of the roving guard as she stepped out. Her haste had finally caught up to her, but it was a fantasy to think she would get out without conflict. She had known a fight would be impossible to avoid completely. She may have even been looking for one.

She turned slowly to face him drawing her knife as she turned. He would be ready for an attack, but she was carrying an unconscious person. He would assume she could not reach him. He would be on guard, but perhaps not enough.

Alexa's body blocked her face from him until her chest was mostly facing him. She could not see him clearly either, until she was mostly square with him. When their eyes met, the Sergeant looked anything but on guard. What color she could see in the shadows cast by the fire was drained from his face. His brows were knit together as if he was trying to solve some challenging puzzle. He was not ready for whatever caused his confusion, but he was not alone.

One of the roving guards was standing next to the Sergeant-At-Arms. He was struggling with something as well. His struggle nearly distracted him from the burden the two shared between them. Suspended between them, held up by her underarms, was a familiar form. Roark recognized the red hair and felt her breath catch. The slight form they dragged toward the tent Roark had just left was Reva.

Anger bubbled up in the Guardian. Her right hand tightened on the hilt of the knife and she began to relax her hold on her burden. She was sizing up each man as she moved to get free from her burden. Trying to escape and take on both men would overwhelm her. She had to free Reva from their grasp.

The roving guard looked from her to the Sergeant with his mouth open. A question was clearly forming on his mouth.

Roark gave them no more time to figure anything out. Whatever had caused their confusion was to her advantage. More than once she had won the initiative because her opponent was surprised by something she could not understand. Reva looked up from her supposed unconscious position and winked at her.

Roark didn't hesitate.

She flipped the knife in the air next to her leg, caught the blade carefully, and flicked it at the Sergeant. With a twist of her body she continued the motion of lowering Alexa to the ground. The light-weight killer drove into the Sergeant's larynx ending any ability he had to argue. She knew from experience that he was drowning from his own blood. It was not a killing strike and she hated that he would suffer until he died. However, it had stopped him from shouting an alarm and was the best attack she could mount with her left hand so occupied. She continued to lower Alexa to the ground.

Reva took advantage of the attack. As the roving guard moved to draw his weapon and abandoned his hold on her, an alarm formed on his mouth. Her form vanished between them in a blur of red hair that was replaced immediately by a small fox. When her paws touched the ground, she bounded into the air at the guard's face.

Incapacitated by even further surprise, he struggled to keep his mind present and draw his sword completely.

When her front paws were near his throat, she transformed again in another blur of red. Her full form flashed into view for just an instant as her knife cut across his larynx, ending his scream before it could fully form. Blood and foam gurgled from the gash that ran across his neck.

Her momentum carried her to the top of his head, transforming again. She landed on his forehead in her fox form and clawed her way over his head, onto his back, and down onto the ground.

Roark herself spent a moment flat footed and exposed as she stood amazed, watching her furry tail scurry away into the dark that obscured the rest of the camp. Before she could lose too much of the advantage, Roark focused again.

Her right hand found another knife as she finished setting the unconscious Alexa onto the ground. Her left knee was touching the ground and Alexa. The Sergeant's hands had come up to his throat where he was groping at the knife trying pull it free and failing as he could not get a breath. An arrow, fired from point-blank range, split his spine and ended his struggle. Blood streamed out of his chest around the exiting shaft that had pierced his heart. He dropped to his knees and pitched over onto his face.

Roark raised another knife into a throwing stance from her knelt position looking for another target. She knew she had no choice now. She would be forced to engage the camp. The cook and piper were crying the alarm as she turned to focus on them. The peace of the night was shattered.

Like a twig snapping in the woods, Roark stood, stepped around Alexa while swapping her knife over to her left hand. In another step she was drawing her sword. The cook was closer to her and armed. Her throwing knife took him in the chest and stopped him where he stood. The piper was standing up and trying to get to a sword that was wrapped up in his other gear at his feet. With two steps and a lunge she closed the distance and drove her sword into the piper before he could free his blade.

Staying out of his reach, she withdrew her sword from his chest while pivoting toward the cook who was staring at the blade that was killing him. She dispatched him with the upward slice of her withdrawal from the piper's chest that cut across the cook's throat.

Her goal of just walking out of the camp was lost. Now she had to deal with the alarm that was running through the camp. There was no way they had not heard the melee that had just broken out in the center of the camp, but there were only five of the roving guards ready and armed to fight, anyone else would be less prepared, for now.

Based on the timing, the roving guard would mostly be to the east. The resting guards would rely on them to keep her at bay while they pulled on sufficient gear. It would not be long before they were all up and after her so she had to strike while they were still arming. She took a breath and waited for the reality of the situation to become clear. Fights rarely came with opportunities to breathe, but she had time to see how they were going to approach her. She was exposed in the light of the fire in the center of the camp.

The noise of the camp around her filled her ears as if sound had just returned to them. There was motion to the east. Occupants of tents there were clambering for gear and she knew the same was happening to the west. A single voice was rallying troops, guiding the roving guards to descend on her. The voice demonstrated the reliable command of an army. She could not overlook the professionalism of what she faced. To assume they would react like a gaggle of brigands after she punched them in the nose would get her killed.

The towers would now be looking inward. Would their height advantage be enough or were they too far out of range? An answer to her question thudded into the middle of the fire. The arrows burned away from the shaft that was helping the archer up there range in on her. She had to keep them reacting to her.

Resistance was weakest to the west. She turned her back on the approaching guards from the east and grabbed up a flaming log from the fire. With an underhand toss, the torture tent was ablaze in a woosh as the oil treatment caught. The fireball highlighted the troops to the west. Many stood in the sudden light, donning armor or clothing, staring at the sudden death that had descended on their camp. Some, who were less surprised were sneaking toward her and cursed at the sudden exposure. An archer who had been tracking her had his bow drawn back to the ear. Her skin pricked and tingled as she ducked and hoped for a lucky glancing blow. An arrow flashed past her shoulder as she ducked. The shaft thudded into the archer's chest. Control and concentration lost, he released his pent up weapon. The arrow flashed away into the night as he fell backward no longer tracking her.

Two men skirted around the flaming tent and bracketed Roark. Running footsteps raced up behind her as the rovers, fully armed and alert, charged for her. From her crouch, she aimed and threw another knife ending a sneaking guard from the west's approach and causing his partner to fall back a step.

Freed to adjust to the fresh attackers, Roark turned in her place and met a falling sword with the middle of her own blade. She tilted it away to allow her attacker's momentum to carry him away from her and toward the flaming tent in a stumbling fall. Metal skated across metal throwing sparks out around them. Because she had allowed her attacker to fall away from her and had not resisted the blow, she still had her sword up for an attack as the second charging guard reached her.

She swung her blade down across his body in a quick slice that cut through chain links, leather armor, and gambeson. His chest opened up as ribs surrendered to the harsh blow. A surprised look replaced the fierce scowl as he died. Roark thanked the fates that her arm had not failed her.

Someone beyond the growing circle of light was coaching the fighters to be careful. He told them to fall back. He wanted them to form a line to encircle the invader. With the eastern guards starting to get organized it was a reasonable plan, and he was reacting to it.

Roark could not allow that. She focused out into the darkness. The man who was organizing the troops was following the three remaining roving troops. Behind them, the soldiers at the tents were arming themselves and throwing on recently discarded armor. Roark had to attack now.

An arrow thudded into the ground beside Roark. Closer. One of the "tower" guards was starting to zero in. She had to get out of the light.

She drew a fighting knife as a companion to her sword and fell back toward the western line of tents. Some lightly armed men tried to form a wall to stop her. In a few strides she was across the space. Compared to her, they seemed to be moving too slowly. Her sword drove into the exposed chest of the nearest. She bent her arm and stabbed around the dying man to take another attacker in the neck with her knife.

Her right hand extracted the sword smoothly and her left pulled the knife through the muscles of the dying man's neck to rip out his throat. Stopped where she was, Roark bent her knees slightly and jumped over the next few soldiers.

She landed behind the line and turned her back on the tents to face the four other soldiers who had made it clear. A fighter that had predicted her move was already turned to face her and dropping his sword to cleave her through the shoulder and on across her body. She could not get her sword up in time. She cringed to prepare for the blow she knew was going to land.

His blade struck hard against her leather armor and Roark wished for an instant that it was plate armor. The blade glanced off of her shoulder with a loud ringing clang throwing the warrior off balance. Confused by the outcome that she expected to kill her, it took her a moment to react. Her attacker was also surprised and slow to react. Roark thrust her knife into his ribs, and she heard his cry of pain and surprise as his life ended. He had known after his attack had failed that he was in trouble, but she had been faster. In the end all he could do was try to spin away. It had almost been enough, but she had driven the knife deep into him and his momentum ripped the knife from her grip leaving her with only her sword.

The fire in the tent was providing light to the western side of the camp in flickering orange-red waves. She retreated away from the three remaining soldiers on that side and slipped toward the northern most tent. It brought her closer to the northern "tower" guards, but they would not be able to see her.

She was out of knives. That had been the last of her longer dueling knives. No one was venturing into the circle cast by the cooking fire or the tent. Roark knew most of the remaining forces were holding to the east side of the camp. The man rallying the troops was calling the men down from the "towers". He suddenly understood they were useless up there for defending the courtyard in the dark.

Keeping her back to the outside wall of the tent, Roark slipped around to the eastern side of the camp. She focused into the darkness to find her enemy. A tingle rippled across her body and suddenly she could see them. Glowing forms appeared in the darkness and quickly became the outlines of men lurking in pairs trying to find her. They had finally formed a line and were working toward the middle of the camp. The closest pair were walking around the front of the tent she was behind.

With caution, she stepped out to the left side of their line. She knew it would expose her, but she needed to whittle down their odds. She didn't know how she could see them, and worried that the wizard had somehow illuminated them all. She had completely forgotten about him since she had not seen him in the camp, but had to consider he was helping everyone see better.

The line passed her. The sudden ability to see was apparently unique to her. Taking advantage of their flanks and inability to see her, she grabbed her nearest attacker by the throat and lifted him off the ground. Her sword would not help her, so she dropped it. Grabbing the man by his waist she dug her fingers into his neck and ripped the larynx and most of his throat away. He fell away from her as she stepped to her right to repeat the kill on the next man in line.

Having silently dispatched the far end of the line designed to wrap around her, Roark paused to look at the glowing figures. A flitting movement at the far end told her that Reva was still engaging the enemy.

The small fox form skittered around them without touching anyone. It paused behind one and then formed into the glowing figure of Reva. A knife thrust into the back of each man's head and then she was a fox again and moving on. Roark joined her in dispatching what remained of the camp until all that remained was the third in command.

"Keep moving up," he whispered as if the line was still on either side of him.

Roark and Reva walked next to him as he approached the lighted circle. He looked left and right as he started to step forward and recognition dawned on his face. The firelight exposed them all and fear replaced the recognition. Reva drove her knife into his side, Roark raked her right hand across his neck. Their final opponent crumpled to the ground.

The roar of conflict died away from Roark's ears and she listened for any opponents while she scanned all around the camp. All she could hear were the whimpering cries for mercy and groans of those who were unlikely to survive much longer.

All that remained of the enemy were eight men circling down from the high walls of the ridge around them. Roark didn't want to fight them. The fight was over, and she wanted to collect her prize and leave this valley.

"Hear me!" she shouted into the night. "Anyone who lives in this valley, I give you your lives if you can save it and leave here now. If you come into this camp or harass me further, I will kill you as I have killed the rest. Look around. Consider your strength. Leave and never come back here."

Roark peered into the walls of the ridge and picked up the glowing forms of the other soldiers, pairs picking their way along the dark path to the ground. They all stopped and seemed to be discussing their options. A few individuals on the valley floor were slinking away from the camp.

"Leonas, are you down there?" a voice called from the western side searching for someone in charge. Silence answered his query. Roark let the call settle into the crackling fire that was consuming the remnant of the tent. Either Leonas was dead, or he was choosing not to answer. The result was the same. Roark answered the third call.

"There is no one down here that is your ally. Leave here. Never come back. Never work for wizards again." Roark called up to him.

She watched as the realization dawned on them and they turned back to walk up to the top of each ridge. Roark watched until the forms disappeared from view.

In the dark, Reva stepped up next to her and grinned. Her vision still shimmered with the glow of every living person as well as the bright glow of the fire. Reva looked odd in her vision but it was clear that she was smiling for some reason.

"What do you find so pleasing?"

"You are not what you seem to be at all, Guardian."

"Neither are you, Scout." She pointed to Alexa who still lay where she had placed her before the fight had escalated. The question on Reva's face did not have to be asked. The remnant of the tent she had carried Alexa from and the absence of Elsa was answer enough.

Together they walked over to the still unconscious woman. Roark knelt next to the woman and brushed the hair that fell into her face out of the way. She was breathing deep breaths. It was probably the first time she had rested since they had taken them from the camp.

"I need to look around here, I don't want to move Alexa. Can you find the Princess and bring her back here?"

Reva looked up at a branch to the east where a large owl sat watching them. Its white plumage and black dots stood out in a beautiful pattern. "I think she is already on her way."

~~~

Roark followed her gaze up to the limb where the owl perched. It didn't move. It didn't look away. For a moment, Roark thought it was waiting for her to say or do something. Just as Roark was about to look back to Reva, the bird cocked its head to the left.

Roark could not hold back the hysterical laugh. There was more to that bird. Reva knew it. Roark laughed deeper to relieve the stress of the realization that she had been manipulated. She had been traveling with a witch the whole time, perhaps an entire coven.

"Why do you laugh?"

Roark stifled her laugh and let her face settling to a scowl. "I will not be played with any longer."

Reva mirrored the owl's movements as if they both had questions for her. "Played with. You are the one playing with us, are you not?"

They both looked at each other with a tilt to their heads and unanswered questions. Roark recovered first.

"I'm not the one changing forms, becoming a fox, or an owl to watch the carnage like the silly tales of frightened children lost in the Spine. Witch's tricks to beguile." Her hand made a sweeping movement that encompassed Reva and the Owl.

Reva laughed this time. For the first time since they had met, Roark actually felt her anger flare with the young girl she had come to love. She did not like the feeling of being deceived.

"Why do you treat me so? What deception are you perpetrating on me? What do you hope to get from me? This has cost the life of many brave guardians already and one of your own as well. You can't continue to pretend you don't know what is going on. Those who chase you are after more than the princess' body."

Reva realized the gravity of Roark's accusations and became serious.

"I am as confused as you are about those wizards and you. You accuse us of perpetrating some deception, and yet you stand here like this. What deception do you hide?"

Roark held her tongue. The tone of the girls question surprised her, but Reva continued.

"You, the one who I just observed not only sneak into an enemy camp by transforming into a strange man she had never seen before, but at the moment of being discovered took on the form of the very Sergeant-At-Arms who was accosting her."

Reva stepped a little closer to Roark as if to inspect her. Roark almost expected her to touch her to verify she was really standing there. She didn't respond to her question because she had no idea what she was talking about. She let her face demonstrate exactly how little she understood.

"You are telling me that you don't know. You are unaware that you actually shift your form?" It was Reva's turn to be quietly stunned. It gave Roark an opportunity to respond.

"I'm not the one changing forms," she said more harshly than she really intended. "You are the shifter, running about in the form of a fox and this..." Roark's retort lost energy like a sail that had lost its wind. She had been trying to understand what the girl was saying even as she responded and was beginning to understand her concerns.

"Have you never realized?" Reva asked with a tone that seemed consoling and filled with pity, almost motherly. "You don't know that you do it." She answered her own question with a trailing voice.

Roark took a step back from the girl who was now staring at her as if she were something odd or strange.

"I don't... I'm not... I... What are you saying?"

"She's saying that you change forms. She is saying that you are a changeling much like she is. She is saying that you don't even know you do it."

Roark turned to look across the lit courtyard between the tents. Cinnia was standing just inside the ring of light. She was dressed in a striking white dress and as clean as she was the first day she had seen her. She was almost glowing in the dwindling light of the fire.

Roark looked from the woman up to the owl who still sat on the limb watching them and then back. She felt weak, as if the wizard was back and manipulating her with his magic.

"What deception is this? I know you are playing with magic, but you talk of things that are not true. I am nothing more than what I appear to be."

Cinnia didn't move closer. Reva looked on but didn't speak.

"That is a true statement, I'm sure, but you don't even know what that means. Roark, that's not your real name is it?"

"It's how I'm known. It's my name."

"But you took it… from someone else… to protect yourself. Didn't you?"

Roark didn't answer.

"Think about it. Dara showed me a great deal about you. Not intentionally of course, she could never do that, but she showed me how to find out and while you traveled here I looked into what she revealed."

Roark felt fear like she had never known. What kind of trap was this?

"Your name is Edana, isn't it?"

"I'm Roark."

"Yes, to protect yourself, you are Roark. The greatest guardian the Spine has ever known. A great warrior at seventeen. Greater than any legend ever told in fact. Your reputation is so good. You have changed how the world looks at Guardians."

"That's well known. That's who I am."

"But…"

"There is nothing more," Roark answered, feeling the lie burn her chest. She *had* to protect the secret.

Cinnia stepped forward waving her hands from her hips into the light toward Roark. She raised her arms to block whatever she was throwing her way. Whisps of smoke from the burning tent flowed toward her and then took form. Movement in the smoke figures played out the scene she knew by heart. Her sister lay broken across the chest. Her attackers laughed and jostled one another as smokey reminders of the past.

The chest opened slightly. Roark remembered how heavy it had been. Her young muscles struggled to lift it until she had grown angry and afraid. Then it had opened.

Her sister's body fell to the floor drawing the attention of the attackers. She had not wanted them to know she was there. She had hoped they were gone already, but they weren't. Before they could understand what was happening, Roark was out of the chest and across the small room stabbing a makeshift dagger into the chest of the closest one. She couldn't remember where she had found the weapon.

She heard the voice of the apparition call her name. "Roark!"

But it wasn't her name yet. They had not expected her. The companion who had shouted was grabbing the youth she had stabbed. Even in the carved smoke face she could see the pain and anger. She had seen it so many times on the faces of others who had seen their loved ones killed.

"You killed Roark," he shouted.

He reached for his sword. She ducked her head and drove her shoulder into his chest. She didn't look as small as she had been in the smoke. She didn't even look like a small girl like she had been. There was something wrong with this vision of the past. She had been a small girl. She had not expected to be able to move him, but she had. He flew across the room and slammed in to the wall with a wet thud. He dropped to the floor and didn't move. The noise was drawing others to the room, Edana had to run. She had to get away. She had to escape, but how.

Her smokey form picked up the boy who was obviously larger than she was and dropped him into the chest. Looking back at the other boy on the floor, she quickly grabbed a small silver mirror from her sister's table and looked at her own face. With careful, but quick adjustments of makeup she changed. Someone called out for the pair left behind in the room. She allowed silence to answer them and continued her work. Looking between the boy in the chest and the knocked out "guardian," Edana transformed herself into Roark for the first time.

"You took his place. The other boy had been injured and died a week later. You took your revenge on the others one at a time, but you changed that band into protectors of the innocent in the Spine like they were supposed to be. You created real Guardians."

Edana relaxed her shoulders and allowed the secret out with a sigh. "Yes."

"But, you never knew, or realized, you are magical?"

"I'm not."

Cinnia smiled at her and then at Reva.

"Do you know what I am, Edana?"

"Obviously you are a witch."

"In the understanding of this region, I suppose that is correct. I'm an enchantress. Dara was lost here long ago because she had no champion like yourself. I am at risk and I need you, but it seems we are only going to get out of this if we are all more honest with each other. You need to know everything I know, and you also need to know what you really are."

Edana nodded at the enchantress, realizing that there was something else at work.

"Is it true that you don't know your origins?"

"Yes. I was always just a child in my father's house with a sister and mother until Roark's band of guardians attacked us. After that, I became him as best I could."

"And it didn't surprise you that his friends didn't notice any difference."

"No, not at the time. I didn't wait for them to get a better look though. My revenge on them came as soon as an opportunity presented itself."

"We've all observed you in your male form," Cinnia said without moving any closer. She was afraid of Edana. Edana considered that. A witch was afraid of her.

"You convince others because you actually become Roark, a male leader of the only reliable band of Guardians in the Spine. Do you still have your sister's mirror?"

Roark reached into a pouch on the back of her belt and pulled it out.

"Look at yourself."

Roark brought the mirror up to look at herself and felt a burning rush across her body. In the mirror she could see exactly what she expected, her face with streaks of smoke and blood running down it.

"Did you feel it?"

Edana looked past the mirror at Cinnia.

"Did you feel the rush of magic as you changed?"

"Changed?"

"Yes, Edana. You just changed forms. I watched you do it, as did Reva."

The young girl nodded her head indicating she had watched it as well. Edana didn't believe them.

"When you change, I also watched the magic flow across your body. I watched you change in two ways."

"How do I know you tell the truth? You are a witch. You have lied to me through this entire journey."

"I am not the only one who has lied."

"I have not lied to you."

"You have lied to yourself. Ask yourself, what do I gain by deceiving you about this? What can I hope to gain by making you think you are magical and can shift your shape?"

Edana considered the question almost even as Cinnia posed it. What would she gain? What benefit would she get?

"I cannot say. I do not know what benefits witches gain from their trickery," Edana spat out the quickest defense she could find even though she didn't feel it.

"How can I prove this to you? You have fooled yourself for so long, I'm not sure you even realize what happens when you fight like you just did. Perhaps you will believe Reva. She is certainly not a witch. She had never deceived you, not even when I needed her to."

Roark considered that for a moment. The girl had never lied to her that she knew. She had never told her of her ability to change forms as she did, but she had never lied.

"If she swears on whatever magic created her, I will believe her."

Reva smiled at Edana. "I swear on my magical soul. I swear on anything you require. I swear on my love for you."

Edana felt a twinge of pain. It lasted for a moment and then changed into a burst of happiness. The girl chose to admit her feelings and then use them as a guarantee of her honesty. Edana's hand rested on her heart, and she smiled at the girl.

"Then tell me, what did you observe."

"My love, I watched you take several forms this night and others. But tonight you took multiple forms to take on these soldiers that lay at your feet. Many of them faced a creature of legend that none have seen in ages. When they saw you, many lost their nerve to fight."

"Your strong arms bristled with a scaled ridge. Your obsidian talons rent flesh when your sword failed you. Weapons glanced off of your scaled hide. You, beautiful creature, were a dragon if ever one walked the Spine."

~~~

Edana sat down as if someone had severed the strings that held her up.

She didn't look at either of the women who stood staring at her. They shared quick glances and then continued to watch her cautiously.

She looked at her hands, which were speckled and streaked with blood and dirt. In the flickering light of the fires it was hard to tell which was which.

Those hands were the gentle delicate hands that could give her away among her men. They were the hands she often hid in her bulky overtunic or kept busy to avoid the chance anyone was looking.

There was nothing to say. Each part of her screamed that she was a young woman, the same young woman who had hid among the clothes to save herself instead of protecting the ones she loved.

She was the weak one. She was dependent on her father to save her from the invaders, until the night he failed, the one night she needed him to protect them all.

A warm tear fell from her cheek, burning her skin as it reminded her of her failure, that night among the clothes hidden until the screaming stopped. Hidden until she had to come out for fear she would suffocate in the chest and no one would find her.

Even now she continued to hide among other men for safety. There was no way she was some magical creature of legend. There had to be a mistake. She was not...

She shook her head at the impossible. She knew who, and what she was, even though she had almost forgotten that name. Even though she had forgotten the family and past she had abandoned that night. That night she had fled the village for the last time. The night she had met Dara and faced the future she had never sought or wanted.

Her home had been destroyed by those everyone trusted to protect them. It was the first time a child had learned the meanings of betrayal. It was the first time Edana had discovered that she could trust no one. The sting of betrayal now resurfaced as if new. It threatened to unleash feelings that she had locked away. Feelings that pushed at the box and promised to upset her delicately balanced sanity; her safe facade that protected her.

Edana looked up at Cinnia.

"How?"

"You did what you had to do, even then. You killed most of the men who chased you to the valley. You forgot most of that. You've built quite an elaborate false memory around that night and the years that followed. Dara tried to warn you. She tried to tell you when you came to her what the outcome would be. She tried to warn you away from the path you had already chosen. The path you will always chose. Your noble birth allows no less of you."

"I'm just a young girl, trapped in this horrible place. I've done what had to be done."

Cinnia approached cautiously and sat down next to her. Looking warily, the Princess put her arm around Edana's shoulders.

"That you have, Edana. You have changed the Spine in a way that none but one expected."

"Dara knew, she tried to tell me that night."

"Yes, and again recently she tried, but…"

"But?"

"You are a very magical being."

Edana shook her head even as she realized the truth behind that statement.

"You created a fantasy to protect yourself. No witch or enchantress could break it. You are the only one who can break the illusion of the past that you have woven."

"I like my life. I liked it… until you came here and brought the trouble back."

Cinnia looked down at her own lap. "I know it seems that way, but the realms beyond the Spine still exist. The evils that came here then remained outside the Spine and grew stronger."

"The trouble was always coming back." Edana stated it as a truth, not a question.

"That's what Dara was trying to tell you. That's what you didn't want to hear so long ago. The path you began with your actions that night would come back around. Now it has, or at least it has begun to."

Edana shrugged off Cinnia's arm and stood back up. As much as she wanted to deny what had happened, she could no longer hide from the truth. It was clear to her now.

She turned to look at Reva, who stood waiting. "You say you saw me transform?"

"Yes."

"How have I remained hidden this long?"

"You haven't," Reva answered looking at her with a sad grin.

"Your actions severed their control in the Spine. The legend of Roark grew quickly and spread throughout the realms. It was impossible to believe, but those who made their fortunes in the passes of the Spine, the ones you had cut off, knew the reality of it. They could no longer maintain their profits."

"Because of me?"

"Yes, beloved. Since that night when you returned as Roark and took your place at the head of the Guardians, not a single caravan was lost. Men who traded on the suffering in The Spine started losing gold with each caravan."

"I knew that, but I thought…"

"You thought nothing would ever end the corruption in the Spine. You thought none would ever stand for the people abandoned here," Cinnia finished her thought.

"You became quite a legend in a short time. You are why we are here," Reva added.

Edana stopped and looked at her. Why were they looking for her? What kind of trap was this they had lured her into?

She took two steps back from the women she was beginning to trust and felt the fear of being manipulated. Her skin prickled with the fire of magic.

"You came here to use me."

She felt her arms grow stronger and her talons extend. They had been telling her the truth about her true nature.

As she stepped back from them, she felt the scales cover her body and the ridge along her back stand up. She was dragon, and the pass was hers. It had always been hers.

"Why are you looking for me? What foul bargain do you wish to make with me? You smell of the wizards that chase you. You are wrapped in the very corruption you warn about."

Edana punctuated her accusation with a deep inhale through her expanded nostrils as her child like face expanded into her long nose. The smell of the dead soldiers around her tantalized her senses.

Her tail swept away from her in agitation as it expanded from her spine. It cast the fire aside, scattering the logs and embers into the night with a shower of sparks. She settled onto her front legs, but her head still hovered above the two women who cowered beneath her. Her sensitive ears picked up the noise farther up the valley as the remaining men raced to escape her. She felt an urge to go after them, to force them to face their crimes that she could smell on them even this far away.

"Why are you playing with me? Do you think it is safe for you to tempt such as me?" Edana's voice boomed through the valley. Her wings spread out behind her in a broad canopy that reflected the firelight from the tent back at them.

Cinnia dropped to her knees immediately and Reva followed her with only a slight delay caused by her amazement at the transformation she had just watched.

"Forgive our arrogance," The Princess called out with her head toward the ground not looking up at Edana. "We meant no disrespect. We came here because we were sent here to die. You were our only hope."

Edana dropped her head closer to the women now kneeling before her.

"Sent here?"

"Yes. I am betrothed to the Prince of Parthia. That is no lie, but my father is using me. He sent me here to die in the passes."

"Why?"

"He is a member of the Wizards Alliance. They fear the power of the Enchantress. They have fought for generations to destroy every enchantress ever born. We threaten them with our strength from birth, so they kill us as we are born. Some of us escape, for a time. The Lord of Parthia and his son protect those within the border of his realm. My union with him will create a realm where the Enchantress' power can again flourish. I have worked hard to secure his love and support without the use of magic even as my father fought against it with every magic tool he had."

"So, your father sent you here to die. You knew you were condemned, so you sought me out to help you."

"I did not seek you out. We were destined to meet. The day you stood up, our paths were destined to cross. There is no other outcome possible. Dara saw that even then."

Edana dropped her head closer to the woman and let her nostril rest just above the ground. Her eye could take in the whole form of the woman kneeling where she was. The Princess looked up from her position and into Edana's great eye with respect but no fear.

"You, and that witch, conspired to force my hand. You played games to get me to help you."

"No."

Edana smelled no deception. She was telling the truth.

"Then what do you call this elaborate ruse to cause me to take up your fight?"

"It is no ruse. Dara is a sister. She was sent here to die in a similar way. They never expected her to escape the caravan she was in. She has defied them for many years and her escape started this possible path to you. She became the witch of the Spine that they had consistently told everyone to fear and taught them time after time they were no match for her. Now, they fear her and make everyone else fear her."

"But they don't fear me?"

"They don't know about you. They know of Roark the powerful guardian, not you. There are rumors that you are not human. There are rumors that you are a rouge wizard. There are tales that are beginning to surface of your other abilities, but it is still only legend and rumor. No one knew you were a woman, a female. No one had put together the signs. I suspected but didn't realize what the scrying was telling me until I talked with Dara. She knew."

"So, what do they want. Why are you here?"

"They sent me here to die, just like Dara, but they wanted to use me to draw you out in order to kill you. You've cut off their profits and minimized their power in the Spine. They want you dead, and I was sent to give them the chance to solve two problems at one time."

"Hmmff." Edana huffed her disrespect into the dirt of the valley floor.

"They hoped that I would also draw out Dara, which I'm afraid we have done."

"But she knew that was going to happen. That's what she accused me of so long ago."

"Yes, I think we all knew she would not last forever standing against them. That night when she met you, she had hoped that she could help you learn and maybe even convince you to help us."

"But, I can stop them."

"No!" They were the first words Reva spoke since Edana's transformation and they were laced with emotion and passion Edana had not felt before. Her head turned slightly to face the young girl.

"You can't face them when they stand together," she said with fear apparent both on her face and her scent. "They have more power than you when they are together. They will destroy you." A tear dripped from the girl's cheek. "We have all faced their tyranny, and when they stand together few can withstand them."

Edana nudged the girl with her chin gently. The simple caress resonated in her very scales and tingled like the magical fire across her whole body. She loved this one. The small one felt the same for her.

The tingling transformed into the magical fire that rushed over her, the harbinger of her change, and the collapsing of her form began. She could not remember the last time she had been in her full form, there had been no need for it since she had hatched. She had needed to stay out of site, and now was no different.

She had needed to stay in her human form, to help them. It was not time for her full form yet.

It took several moments for her massive body to collapse, and neither woman moved as she returned to a form familiar to them all. As her forelegs returned to arms, she stood up and placed her now soft palm on the cheek of the changeling she was in love with.

"You are a wise and tricky one. Was this your idea or hers?" Edana looked over at the Princess who was standing again and looking at the new form before her.

"We are all part of this. I give advice to my Lady as asked."

"Of course you do," Edana noted. "So, we can't help Dara. How do we help you?"

"Get me to Parthia."

Edana looked around the camp that had invaded her realm. They had paid this night, but they still acted as if they owned it. She had fought to minimize their control in the Spine, and now she needed to drive them out again.

The Wizards Alliance had joined against her. She had known that powerful hands had played games in the passes, but she had never been able to discover who had been behind the actions that had poisoned her realm and tormented the people who lived within it. It was time to stand and take the fight to them. It was time to end their control in The Spine, then maybe she would see how they liked losing control of their own realms. This day, as Dara had predicted, Edana would stand against the wizards and remind them why this realm was named as it was.

She faced Reva and Cinnia who were watching her with concerned faces. She thought a moment about all that she had learned and decided and looked at her allies. With a moment of concentration, she thought about the form she had hidden for so long and brought it forward in her mind. She thought of her sister who had died at their hands, and others who had been victims of their actions. A fiery tingle ran across her body, but this time she knew what she was doing. She focused on the image in her mind and, as if she drew every detail on a canvas, she created the form she would take from then on. In the flickering light her glimmering black armor covered her from shoulder to thighs. Her leather boots shined in the glow of the flames. At her waist she wore her belt of knives. From her shoulder hung her bow and her quiver of arrows crested with white fletching. Her dark hair fell to her waist in braids that twisted together in a single thick plait. Atop her head she wore a helmet of polished black metal with a crest of dragon's scales that ran across the crown and down the back to form a protective plate over her neck. On either side of her hips she carried her long sword and long fighting knife in black lacquered scabbards.

A smile crossed her face as she let her female characteristics emerge.

"Edana died in that chest with my sister. I am Roark who rose from her death. The man who had that name before died as well, but I will forever be Roark, Guardian of the passes of the Dragon's Spine. Today, I take the fight back to those who abuse my realm." She drew the ebony blade of her sword to punctuate her oath and raised its shimmering blade into the night sky.

~ ~ ~

Edana sheathed her sword and faced her charges.

"I need to know all of the details of your plan. I need to know who I'm facing. Tell me all of the members of this guild of wizards that you know. Too long they have walked this realm and taken advantage of those who live here. I am the champion of those who have suffered at their hands, and I will exact their price from those who have taken advantage of them."

It was clear on Cinnia's face that she was conflicted. This was not the first time Roark had seen a similar look when she had threatened or challenged those similar or close to her.

"Your father. You worry that I judge him among those who are guilty of these charges." Roark didn't flinch from the truth but Cinnia did.

"He…"

"Don't defend him. You may struggle with this allegiance, but no matter how twisted your commitment to him is, he has attacked me directly. For you, I will give him room to change his mind ask my forgiveness for his assault of me and my realm. You can carry those tidings to him once I've saved you and delivered you from him, but that is between you and your betrothed. I give him a year from the day you are delivered. After that, I hunt him among his kin."

Cinnia stared at her. Her voice seemed lost in the revelation that her father was the target of a magical creature on a hunt.

"She will do as you suggest. You are most generous to give him this opportunity," Reva answered prodding Princess.

Cinnia's frown turned against her lady-in-waiting. Reva looked at her with the softening look of an ambassador warning her liege to take the deal before her. Cinnia nodded her ascent and finally found her own voice.

"It is kind of you to consider my concerns as you do. You have read my worries well. I had hoped to stand against my father from the safety of a new realm with the support of its king."

"You will be lucky if you survive to see that realm. You overestimate your strength here. You have intentionally brought death to my realm with intent as raw as your father's. You are lucky I don't leave you here for them to find you and do with you as they wish, but that would require me to go back on my word."

Cinnia wanted to rebuke her, but realized she was not in a position to make any arguments. Instead she swallowed her protest.

Roark nodded at her realization and respect. "Are you ready to complete this journey?"

"Yes," was her simple reply.

"Dara was wrong."

"Why do you say that?"

"She accused me of making a decision that damned her. You made that decision. I was simply the tool. The wizards wanted her destroyed, and they used you as the tool to make that happen. If they have succeeded, you paid for that. I will not take responsibility for her, that is between you and her other sisters. She can't see you at fault because you both see yourselves as victims in this, but your decisions forced this to happen, here in the Spine. You could have fought this anywhere else, but even you see this realm as a place where you can manipulate people and events. I will not allow that anymore. Be careful, sisters, that you don't find yourselves in the same place as your brothers. This realm is not your's to control any more than it is their's, not anymore."

Cinnia obviously wanted to argue, to say that she had no choice. But she held her tongue. Reva watched her reaction with obvious concern. She knew Roark's point was correct, and that she had a right to call her mistress on her actions. Roark turned her back on them as they collected themselves.

"Take care of your lady," Roark advised over her shoulder with contempt, "She deserves better for her sacrifice. Her mind is your duty, Princess. You used her as sorely as you used me and this realm. This is all on your soul."

With her comments left to the night breeze, she turned toward the tent she wanted to search since she had entered the camp. She crossed the dark space to it and pulled the flap open.

It was mostly empty except for a single folding style desk that fit into the chest that sat next to it. The wizard expected to come back here.

She crossed over to the desk and sat at the stool that gave the man a perch to command from. As she settled there, the allusion to birds continued to fill her mind. She thought of Cinnia, but the image she felt in every corner of the tent was of a raven, not the owl Cinnia had used.

A cage in the corner, covered by a cloth and hidden in the shadows, drew her attention. She drew back the cover expecting to find the very raven she sensed but found the cage empty. She knew this wizard now. He would be in black and look like his familiar.

She continued her search of what he had left. On the table a single black feather quill sat on the table next to a book. She knew it would not be his spell book. He would never leave that behind. He would never carry it out from his keep. She turned the page back a leaf and looked at the scribbled, coded message on the page. It was the same as what the spy had used to encrypt his notes.

She looked up to where Cinnia would be standing beyond the flap of the tent. She had said Alexa could decode the message. Not likely now or any time soon. But what had she meant?

Roark narrowed her eyes a little as she considered her question. Did she know the code of the wizards, or did she know who pursued them? She hated distrusting the woman who she was protecting, but she couldn't help but think they might be even deeper in the control of the wizards themselves.

She turned away from the table and stepped out into the night again. Reva looked over to her as she stepped out of the tent and their eyes met. Even without speaking Reva knew she needed her and moved in her direction.

They met half-way between the tent and the fire ring. Cinnia was speaking softly to Alexa, who was awake but nowhere near able to talk about her experience in the camp where she had been tortured. Roark groaned at the pain that woman had experienced and was still reliving.

"She is strong." Reva said as she joined Roark.

"Not that strong."

"That bad?"

"A sight I'll never forget, and the worst I've seen even among the horrible crimes I've witnessed in The Spine."

Reva only nodded. There was no need to argue about something she had not seen.

"I need to ask you a question," Roark probed.

"Whatever you need."

"Why do you travel with the Princess? You don't need their protection. You obviously are able to take care of yourself."

Reva smiled, "I am, but you never know the things that will happen on your path. I've benefitted as much from their company as they have mine."

"But…"

"For many good reasons, you don't trust others very well. But, I can tell you that these women are trustworthy."

Roark looked at her with an accusing look.

"You are, of course, correct that they have used this realm and you. It is sad that it was ever allowed. But that is not completely their fault."

Roark paused to consider the girls words. She seemed much older than her appearance indicated. Roark still didn't feel like she had the whole story, and that was a threat to her survival.

"Why can Alexa decrypt the wizard's code?"

"Cinnia's father has her encode all of his messages."

Roark just looked at her. She couldn't help but feel that this proved this was more of a setup. They worked with Cinnia's father. They knew he was a wizard. They admitted that he intended to kill them all. They were protecting him.

"They, She is the Princess' lady-in-waiting. She has to serve the royal house. All of them."

"But, how can he trust her. She knows his code and can translate messages he sends to anyone. How could he trust his code is safe when he knows they are fighting against him?"

"It is a complex code that requires a book to decode it."

Roark didn't understand why that mattered.

"She doesn't have his book with her. He never lets it out of his control."

Roark still didn't understand more than that Reva was trying to explain why her question was so unimportant.

"She decodes and encodes his messages with his book. She doesn't really need his book because she never forgets anything she reads. That's the secret he doesn't know."

"So, he thinks his code is safe because she doesn't have his book. But she has it all memorized."

"We've used her ability to save lives before, but we have to be careful to keep him from becoming suspicious."

"How did the spy encode his messages?"

"The king has several different codes in his book. He assigns them out to his spies, and those spies never live long enough to give away the secrets or the code."

"Do you think this wizard is using the same code as her father?"

"Probably not, each wizard creates his own codes. This one is probably different."

"Then we can't decrypt his journal."

Reva shook her head. "Unless he used the wizards common code book."

"Can you translate that?"

"No, I've never needed to. Alexa knows it."

Roark shook her head.

"I had hoped to find out who was following us and how he tracked us so well. We should have lost him.

He had to be using magic to track us, but I've never seen anyone else track like this."

"They are always finding new ways to use magic to follow others. Wizards aren't very good at scrying. Enchantresses like the Princess are better at it. They have developed other ways."

"This was like they had our scent, but they weren't using scent trackers…"

Roark wanted to ask her more but left it alone. As she said, there was something unnatural about how they did it. As she tried to figure out her next move to discover more from the wizard's things, she stuck her fingers into the pouch at her belt and felt the tag she had removed from the beast in the tent. It was a brutal piece of jewelry for a man to wear, but Roark would never call the beast she had killed a man.

She turned the plate she had removed from the heavy chain over in her fingers and examined it. There was a number stamped into the rough oval of metal. It wasn't jewelry, it was a tag and it identified the beast by number. The fact that it took more than two digits to number this one caused Roark's blood to run cold.

"What's that?"

"A tag, worn by the beast that tortured Elsa to death."

Even in the darkness Roark saw the color drain from Reva's face. She swallowed hard even as she tried to hide her response.

"Don't go keeping secrets now. What do you know?"

"Tales, that's all."

"We have the perfect night for it then. We have a camp, a fire, and no where to go till the sun comes up."

Reva looked up at Roark and nearly begged with her eyes. Roark shook her head and held the tag out at her.

"Secrets caused this. Do you want to continue this? I'm going after them with or without what you know. You can save me the surprise by telling me what you know. How can it hurt the Princess more."

"It's not the Princess I'm scared for, specifically. We're all at risk to speak of the golem that represents."

"What kind of amalgam of evil are you talking about?"

"Trackers of the worst kind. Beasts who search for one soul or one type of being. It's up to the wizard who creates the beasts."

Roark took the girl by the arm and walked her over to the circle of light from the fire Cinnia had rescued. The Princess looked up from her care of Alexa to watch them approach. It was clear that she did not understand why Roark was being so harsh. Roark did not allow the fear and concern on her face stop her from finding out the answers she needed.

"Then, I think we should all know what secret you're about to share. Tell us of these golem who wizards such as the Princess' father creates and sends out into the realms to hunt."

GUARDIAN'S REVELATION

Reva looked between the two powerful women. It was clear by her concerned look and nervous demeanor that she did not want to damage the trust between herself and Cinnia. Roark gave no ground. Cinnia, however, shrugged as if to indicate that it was already too late to keep any more secrets.

Roark grinned. Cinnia was correct and she would have to deal with her part in deceiving the Guardian. But Roark also knew she was going to have to stop pushing the Princess about her deception soon, or she would lose her and any help she could offer.

Reva shook her head and warned Roark silently to let her out of the middle. Again, Roark calculated how much longer she could use the guilt to her advantage. It was starting to wear thin. She said nothing to either of them but waited for one of them to explain what they had kept secret.

Cinnia started, releasing her lady-in-waiting from having to abandon her loyalty.

"The *bloodhounds* are magical creations of the wizards. They use them occasionally to find certain people or types of people."

Roark looked at her to indicate that she needed more than that, but the Princess needed no more coaxing. She was going on. She had apparently decided there was no value to farther deception.

"They, my father, takes volunteers of a sort. Followers who are promised an opportunity to be more than they are now. People who are infatuated with magic and the opportunity to use it. Through ceremony and ritual they enhance their senses to the point where they can smell the person or type of person the wizards want them to track."

Roark thought of how the beast in the tent was acting and she felt something had to be missing. She pushed on her point.

"The one in the tent was... frantic... crazed."

"Yes. It's a side effect of the intense sensitivity they are given."

"It," she refused to think of the creature as a man, "was in a sexual frenzy."

"Ah." Cinnia nodded as if she was agreeing to something far less horrible. "I have never had the opportunity to study or observe one of them." She was being cautions not to sound too clinical. She seemed to know that it made her sound heartless. Roark felt her own gorge rise at the thought of what they were doing to people. "But it makes sense," she finished in a whisper.

Roark took that information in and stood looking at the enchantress for a moment. She seemed to know a great deal about them to have never seen one. She wanted to push harder to get more, but something told her all she needed to know was coming.

Cinnia shrugged and went on. "Animals hunt for different reasons. Most are highly sensitive to scent or sight when they hunt for food. Humans are not as attuned to their feeding senses since we have domesticated animals and can farm. The more powerful drive in humans is procreation, and I believe it is primarily because of the pleasure motivation. If I had seen your specimen, I may have been able to verify that theory. It sounds promising given your question. It seems the rituals focus on the procreation drive and they may even be augmented with enhancements of their pleasure centers to increase drive."

Roark was somewhat disturbed with the detached way she discussed what Roark had witnessed in the tent. She could still see the beast's thrusting hips pounding into the dead flesh of what had been a living woman the last time she had seen her.

"You've never seen them when they catch their prey, have you?" she said through clinched teeth.

She shook her head. "No, but I can imagine. Racing dogs that are allowed to catch their decoy often destroy it because of the pent-up passion to catch it. They let their feeding senses go crazy. They never race again, either. It destroys their drive. Game hunters usually don't allow animals who track via hunger senses to catch their prey. There are exceptions, and some that train better than others. I expect humans driven to find something based on their sexual desire, augmented with the promise of physical pleasure, and then enhanced with magic would be quite excited when they caught their prey. I would have expected the wizard to hold off the *bloodhound* to save it though. The release from successful capture would be incredible and would probably keep it from ever being useful again."

Again, her matter of fact conversation around the horrible beast that had ground a beautiful woman into the dirt troubled Roark. The longer she was associated with the Princess the harder it was becoming to like her. The look on her face must have been very transparent.

"Oh, you must think me a monster. I've never seen one of them or created one myself, but anything that is created through magic is amazing to me. It is captivating of my imagination, and I can regrettably forget that it was used as a horrible weapon. As I said, even if you had not killed it, the creature would never have hunted again, and I'm sure the entire process drives the creature completely mad."

Roark nodded and walked away from the conversation for a moment. The Princess' explanation was understandable, but it was not something Roark was ready to discuss in such a dispassionate way. She remembered how angry the beast had made her and how much she had enjoyed dispatching it. There were very few creatures she felt pleasure at killing. The wizard or all of the wizards were becoming a likely exception to that list. She needed to keep that passion out or she would trap herself. She would lose her edge and her ability to be disconnected from the act. She had to avoid revenge. This was not revenge for her. This was clearing out an invading force. They had to be killed or they would take over her realm and continue hurting those she cared about.

She turned back to the two women. "Gather what you have or need. Help get Alexa ready. We need to get back to Dara's valley. We need her help with Alexa and the wizard who is chasing you."

"There is likely nothing left."

Roark had considered that the wizard had gone off to deal with the witch, but one wizard was no match for one witch. "I'm sure Dara could handle one wizard."

"Wizards don't go after a witch alone. I'm sure he took an army with him and more wizards."

Roark looked around the remains of the army they had fought here and then at Cinnia.

"This is not all of the soldiers wizards have available to them. If he went back for help, and left these soldiers here, he wanted them to guard the prisoners in case we came for them. In fact, he probably hoped to either kill us in the valley with Dara or flush us toward these soldiers to be cut off and ultimately destroyed. He left for reinforcements."

"Then he's coming back here?"

"Not directly."

Roark sensed there was more to that comment and looked at her for clarification.

"I expect Dara had a plan to help you. That's why she knew this was her end. She had foreseen that you would return and make a decision how to proceed. That decision, run or face them here, would decide her fate. If you ran, she would not have to act. If you chose to go against them, she knew they would come after her."

"So, she used herself to draw them away. How long do you think she will succeed?"

"I followed her scrying after the night we met her. They are likely coming back here now."

Roark considered waiting for them and standing here to face them, but she knew this was a place the wizard knew. It was no advantage to her. She considered going after them while they were confident. She was not sure what to do, but she knew how to find out.

"Scry them."

Cinnia thought about her suggestion.

"What do you want to know?"

"Where they are heading. How they will fair."

"Those are two different items. Dara delved into the forecasting of futures. I don't scry that way. I can tell you where they are and what direction they travel. I can't tell you their future plans."

"You said you followed Dara's scrying after we met her."

"I did that to make sure I knew what she had seen. It is too easy to get caught up in all of the possible outcomes and trying to create the outcome you want. It can also get depressing if you don't realize that there is no guarantee that any of your predictions will actually come true. Divination is dangerous to the practitioner."

"So is combat."

Cinnia grinned at Roark. Roark felt the tension and distrust she had for the woman starting to fall of.

"Show me where they are and where they're heading."

Cinnia sat down next to the fire she had carefully rebuilt and adjusted a small pot she found in the remnant of the camp over the flames to encourage the boiling to begin.

They all waited patiently as the bubbling began, watching for the tendrils of truth to start to rise from the water's surface. When these were present, according to legend, the truth could not be obscured and someone skilled at scrying could bring those truths out of the water and force them to show what was happening wherever the witch wanted to see. Some even said, with practice, the witch could get those truths to tell her what would happen in the future.

As the first tendril of steam rose from the pot, Cinnia crushed a series of items together in her hand releasing a pungent aroma. With the aroma lingering, she tossed the batch of components into the water. It flashed and the bubbles became more energetic. The steam rose in larger waves until the figure of the wizard following them developed before their eyes.

The very man they hunted lay sleeping on the ground. He was wrapped against the rain that fell onto his oiled cover which he had pulled up over his head. Roark felt a twinge of satisfaction at his discomfort. It was what a man more comfortable inside among books deserved when he chose to come out into The Spine to try and kill. The wizard avatar fidgeted in its sleep.

"He knows," Cinnia said in a whisper.

"Will he remember. Will he know we did this?"

"Only if he wakes."

Roark considered having her stop. She considered the risk but decided to go on. She needed to know where they were.

"Is there a way to keep him asleep."

"His subconscious struggles with the knowledge that he is being watched, but as an enchantress, I am better at this than he is. He will not wake," she ended confidently.

"Continue. Find out what we need to know."

Cinnia focused and Roark watched her scan the vapors. She waved a hand through the smoky tendrils of people and land. When the smoke turned back into a solid scene, she had adjusted the view above the army. A collection of men slept on a rough ledge above a wash that was running with fresh rain water. Roark could hear the pattering of the rain that fell upon the sleepers. It was soaking the ground and moving slow. Some were unable to sleep in the uncomfortable wet wrappings and simply sat staring at the rushing waters.

Roark grinned. They were enjoying one of the seasonal rains that washed the ridges of the Spine clean. They lasted days when they set in and filled the streams until they would run at shoulder depth. They would not be making it back the way they had traveled out. Roark inhaled the air where she sat. She could smell the petrichor in the air. They were about a day away from them and the rains decided how they were going to deal with them.

"I have seen what I need."

With another wave of her hand, Cinnia shifted the view back to the wizard. She was focusing on something Roark could not see. She waited to see what was keeping her from breaking the contact. The man twitched again and rolled over in his cover. As he shifted, his hand pulled the oil cloth over him and settled again. On the middle finger of the hand that tugged the cloth secure a signet flashed in the smoky image and they both knew that Roark's earlier promise would never be kept. Cinnia looked across the boiling pot and waved a hand through the steam one last time. The figures disappeared and fear filled her eyes. They were wide and pleading for the mercy she had just lost all hope of. Laying there in the full view of them all was her father, King Garth of Arondor.

~~~

Roark crested the ridge leading down into the valley where Dara's small cottage had once rested and stopped. The valley had always been bleak except for the small cottage and shimmering brook that invited her and all others to their death, but now the devastation that replaced it was heartbreaking. The looming gray clouds did nothing to ease the feeling of doom that clung to everything. The rain had paused as if it had wanted to watch them enter the valley, but now it was threatening to start at any moment.

Immediately across the top of the ridge the bodies started. Men, or what had been men based on the basic shape, lay in crumpled piles. Some that had been protected by rock were not so charred, but still they showed signs of their horrible deaths.

The closest one who had sheltered beneath a rock showed the terror of having his breath burned from his lungs as the air around him was engulfed in flame. The remains of his bow, blackened by the fire, lay outside of his shelter where he had dropped it in search of safety. His nearest ally had not found the same safety and his corpse was twisted and gnarled into a knot against the rocky ground. Bone and metal were all that remained. Blackened stumps of trees and brush near him poked up out of the charred ground not taller than ankle height.

The ring of death continued down into the valley telling the story of the overwhelming force the wizards had brought here against Dara. Roark counted the bodies she could see and assumed there were others who had vanished in the extreme heat that swept up from valley floor and over the edges. More than one hundred men had died here when Dara had released her ward.

It seemed that she had waited until they had approached nearly to her door, maybe even through it, before she had released it. Everything within ten ranks of soldiers from her door had been vaporized including her cottage. Nothing stood there. Metal, stone, gems, and other items polished by the fire lay where the soldiers had dropped them. The brook that had passed behind the cottage bubbled in a bloated mournful way. It was the only way Roark knew where the cottage had once stood, and nothing but rock had survived the blast that obviously emanated from it. That rock was slick from the slurry of ash and water that covered it after the rain.

"If I hadn't seen him coming for us I would have believed she had killed him here," Roark whispered in an unintended respect for the death around her.

Cinnia was obviously trying to understand something and gaped at the scene. Alexa still had little interest in the world she walked in, but a smile tickled the edges of her mouth. She had been able to make her way fairly well without much support, but she never spoke and trembled whenever anyone came close to her. Something about this scene was helping her come back from the edge.

Reva, who had been the first to see the destruction in the valley, stood off to the side.

"I've never seen this much power from an enchantress," Cinnia whispered back. "Any enchantress."

"She had a long time to prepare for this. A lot of magical power can be set aside in that time," Roark suggested, not really knowing the mechanics of what she was talking about. "We don't have time to research how she did it, and it seems nothing survived that would explain it. It is clear she wanted them to get close before she took them. Do you think she escaped?"

"I don't even know how she accomplished this. I can't imagine she withstood the magic any better than these soldiers. If she was here, she's gone."

Roark nodded her agreement and started walking down the draws and paths that would take them through the valley avoiding the bulk of the destruction. Their path led across the valley. They would be lucky to make it across before the rains started again, and she wanted to be across the brook before it swelled to a torrent that would swallow them.

On the opposite crest, pleased that the rain had held off, Roark stopped to look back one last time. It told her a great deal about the wizard that had survived. He sent others in to do his work, but she had known that since they had started this dance macabre. He held back and watched from a distance. He never risked his neck in the fray. Roark locked that fact away in her mind as she prepared for the conflict she knew was coming.

"Your father pursues us now. I'm sure he found the clues we left for him, but I need to know... Will he follow us of just send troops to stop us?" Roark broke the long silence of the witch's valley to ask the painful question.

"He will do both," Cinnia responded quickly. Her lack of pause told Roark this was a prepared answer and probably not fully honest. She assumed then, that he would send others first and then follow.

He was running low on eastern troops and it made sense to bring in reinforcements from the west to block them off, if he had any.

"What kind of support do the wizards have in Parthia?"

"Same as Arandor. Most rulers support the wizards. If they don't, bad things seem to happen in most surprising ways."

"Yes, it seems they have a great deal of support everywhere."

Roark let the conversation drop for a while. She needed to think how much support they would get from The Spine. Obviously, they would get some, but could Roark change that? She motioned to Reva to bring her back from her scouting post. Her appearance wasn't immediate, but it was quick.

The spry girl grinned at Roark, knowing she had a plan for the scout, and Roark didn't disappoint.

She increased her stride and the scout matched her with her speed since her legs were shorter. They strode ahead of the other two to create a space where their conversation would not be overheard. Roark knew that Cinna was risking her life, but she didn't know if the Princess fully understood how serious her father was. He was out among the castaways leading the charge. He was already risking himself more than he normally would. Roark had his journal, and both the Princess and Alexa could translate it. The question was if they would. Something told her Cinnia was going to protect her father until the end if she could and survive. It created a much more difficult problem. She laughed at herself quietly, and Reva gave her a questioning look.

She replied with a shake of the head. The problem was no more difficult now than when she first walked into the clearing so many days ago. Now the real complexity of the problem was becoming clear and Roark still felt behind. It was time to change that.

In a whisper nearly as quiet as the wind, "I need for you to find Malich."

Reva nodded but said nothing, understanding Roark's desire to keep the conversation between them.

Roark handed her the message stone they had taken from the spy, and she looked at it with a puzzled look.

"While we were clearing out the wizard's tent early this morning, I wrote it. There were only a handful of outcomes I could predict. This was a long shot, but it was always a possibility that I would need his help."

She nodded again, "What do you want me to tell him?"

"Nothing, just give him the stone. The message tells him everything he needs to know."

"What of My Lady?"

"She does not need to know."

"You put me in a dangerous place."

"Not I."

Reva moaned at the honesty of that statement.

"It could just as easily have been you strapped to that pole in that tent and tortured by that *bloodhound*."

She gravely nodded her understanding, but reserved her agreement. Her face told Roark that she never would have been trapped that way.

"It's not her fault," Roark said to ease the trouble on the girl's face. "She knows her father wants her dead. She knew he would send people to kill her. What she never expected was that he would come himself.

179

That makes this very personal, very hard for her to understand, and very hard for her to accept."

Reva shook her head, a little confused.

"She always thought her father was supporting the wizard's goal to eliminate enchantress blood, but she never expected he was personally committed to the goal and would move against her himself. Now she realizes how he really feels."

"Then there is no doubt what she should do."

"To you and I, that is clear. To her, it is still her father. It would be easier if he had treated her with malice or contempt, but even you can see that he didn't. He is very shrewd. She struggles with her love for him, even as she knows he hunts these passes to kill her."

Reva shook her head and looked at her feet as they walked.

"Can you get away without her knowing?"

Reva looked at Roark and held her eyes before glancing away. The movement was one that Roark had used before, that first day when her men were approaching the Princess' camp. She recognized the intent and casually looked across their path as if she was searching for any sign of an enemy. On a branch ahead of them a white Owl sat watching them walk toward it. Its head was cocked to one side as if it was considering them.

In as low a whisper as Roark could produce, "Can it hear us?"

Reva shrugged imperceptibly to any observer.

"Then I will have to distract her."

This nod was also just a tick to anyone watching them walk.

Roark reached out and placed an arm around the small girl and pulled her against her left side. Reva sunk into her. It was the first time they had touched in days and Roark felt the tingle of desire fill her. She hated that she was sending the girl into danger, but she had no choice. Cinnia had cast this die, now they all had to play out what it cut for them.

The owl lifted from the branch, soared over their heads, and up into the bright sky.

"Go. now," Roark whispered as she leaned down to place a kiss on the girls soft lips. They lingered there together for a moment to reassure each other of their shared commitment to one another. It hurt Roark to release her, but it seemed their show had given Cinnia the impression they needed her to have. "Move up ahead of us, as if I asked you to scout ahead, then double back when you are clear. I'll give you the best break I can."

Reva nodded and skipped ahead of the group in her playful style that the guardian was starting to understand was her most dangerous state.

Roark turned around in her spot and walked purposefully back toward Cinnia and Alexa. Roark could see the owl soaring overhead watching the entire area around them.

"I need for you to tell me your father's weaknesses. What can he not do without? What is he afraid of? I need for you to be explicit and honest with me. It means your life Princess."

Cinna reeled back from Roark's aggressive approach, giving the impression that she was being attacked, even though Roark was only asking her questions. Out of her peripheral vision she could see the controlled spiral of the owl extended and turned into a line.

"Don't act so, Princess. You know you are the only expert here who can tell me what I need to know. You are the only person who knows him."

"I don't know what to tell you, and I will not be talked to in this way."

Cinnia applied her normal regal reaction to any attempt to push her. She pushed back with the expected deference everyone was supposed to give her.

"Put that away, Princess. My respect for you eroded back at the brigand camp where I found Elsa and Alexa bound to be tortured by your father and his *bloodhounds*. Beasts he is probably using right now to track us, to track you. Is that what I need to do? Leave you here for him. He is less than a day behind us."

Cinnia's wall collapsed. Her face showed defeat. Her whole body slumped.

Roark felt a little bad at attacking her the way she was, but she needed her attention squarely focused.

"He never raised a hand against me. Not directly."

"And yet he sent an entire army to kill you, and look what he did to Dara?"

"That is not my fault."

"So you think. From my perspective, you were his tool for accomplishing more than the wizards had in years."

"No. He's chasing me. I'm the threat if I get to Parthia."

"Are you sure your betrothed can be trusted. Are you sure of any of this plan you've created. Every step we've taken has been countered by your father. The only thing that keeps me from thinking you are his spy, is that you are the very thing he is hunting."

Cinnia stopped and stared at Roark.

"Or should I be concerned about that as well."

Cinnia's final resistance failed and her countenance showed it as what strength she had left her and the regal pretense fell. Her final lady-in-waiting stared on, shaking in fear, in her ruined state, providing no support for her Lady. Cinnia was alone for the first time in her life and she seemed to hate the feeling.

"You must hate me."

"I neither hate nor like you Princess. But I have sworn to protect you."

"You can walk away from that contract. It was void on the first encounter with my father and his accomplice wizards. Why do you continue to protect me? He's destroyed Dara, but that still puzzles me. She knew it was coming and still stood there to face him. She said it was because of you, but none of this makes sense any more."

She shook nearly as much as Alexa, and Roark knew she had pushed her a little too far. Maybe it would turn out okay, maybe it would kill them all, but that was the way this contract had gone since the start.

"Why? Why do you continue to help me?"

Roark smiled at the Princess as tears flowed across her still untouched face. "Because I honor my word."

Cinnia stopped and looked at the Guardian. It was as if Roark had smacked her across her face. The Princess stood up straighter. She reasserted her regal bearing.

In a highly respectful show, the Princess curtsied deeply in a formal demonstration of her own respect. At the depth of the motion she looked up into Roark's eyes as she held the stance. The look on her face was very contrite and suddenly submissive.

"You have my word, Guardian. I will do nothing, in any way to stay your hand or affect your work. I will give my full support to you no matter who comes against us. I can give you no more assurance than my word, but as you feel so strongly about yours, I wish to give you that which you respect."

Again, she bowed her head to the Guardian.

Now it was Roark who was surprised. She had not expected the Princess to make such a proclamation. She had cast her as a far less strong person. It took her a moment to get her own bearing back, but when she did, she returned the Princess' curtsie.

"I accept your assurance. You already have mine, and my commitment has never faltered. Thank you, for freeing my hand. I will do only what is necessary to keep you alive, and I already gave you my word to give your father a chance to turn away. I stand by that promise as well."

They both stood together and Cinnia nodded acceptance of the returned respect.

"Then, perhaps you would consider sharing your plan with me. Where have you sent Reva?"

"Princess, with respect, for now, I will keep my own council."

With no further need or ability to keep the Princess off her guard, Roark turned back to her path to the west. The next few days promised to be as hard as those that preceded them, but it seemed all of the pieces were on the board and colored correctly.

GUARDIAN'S PLAN

Roark started the second day of their trek without Reva in a melancholy mood. She knew the scout would return as soon as she accomplished her assigned mission, but she hated for her to be at such risk and alone. Roark was keeping to herself and her plans a secret. Too many times since she met the Princess and started this journey, her plans were known or had been discovered.

Roark no longer thought she might be a spy. Her actions didn't demonstrate the actions of a spy and her promise the day before had been heart felt. Roark understood that she believed what she said. However, there were wizards involved. What the Princess thought might not be the truth.

Believing her promise and trusting her were two very different things. Roark still could not trust that she was not the source, either inadvertently or intentionally, of the information her father was using to track them. Cinnia could scry her father's movements and share, but Roark was not sure that was

185

not a two-way path that helped the wizard as much as it helped them. She had not used that ability again since they had started their angling trek west. The *bloodhounds* were enough of an advantage, she didn't want to help them pinpoint them yet. Knowing they were heading west was enough.

They had broken camp very early and crossed over another challenging ridge. In the afternoon they had crossed a deep river that was at its banks with rainwater to put more challenges between them and their pursuers. Roark wanted information of where they were, but that would have to wait a little longer.

Cinnia joined her as she stood looking down into yet another shallow valley formed by the ridges that gave The Spine its name. They were past the tallest ridge at the middle and were heading down the western slopes as they crossed the parallel ridges. Roark was avoiding passes where spies or brigand bands could be waiting for them. She was not going to make this easy for the man who had been tracking them this long.

Cinna pointed out across the valley to a spot just above the ridge peak. There was a dark dot circling.

Roark looked at her with a quizzical face.

"That is my familiar. You have seen it before in the tree and sometimes following you. Because of that, I have some special abilities with birds. I am connected with that one and can see what it sees."

Roark nodded. She had heard of similar abilities. It was not shocking. She did, however, file away for herself the ability as a reminder that they were working with magical people.

"I've been looking for Reva and she is not out there."

Again, Roark nodded to verify what Cinnia was saying was true.

"Then where is she?"

"I do not know?"

Cinna stared at her in disbelief.

"Where did you send her?"

"I told you, I am not sharing that. What she is doing is critical to our safety."

"But, I can help her."

"I do not know how many more ways your father can discover facts about you. I can't share critical information about the plan with you. Not anymore."

Cinnia took the statement with no argument. "I see the need. You are right. He could be using me. I am not sure how many different ways he has wrapped me in his magic."

"Then trust that I know what I am doing."

"She's right," a voice behind both of them made them jump and turn to face the speaker.

Reva was standing there as if she had not just traveled for two days out and back to deliver Roark's message. She held up her left hand to show Roark that she had a response, and Roark nearly leaped with excitement at seeing it. The obvious joy Roark displayed caused Reva to smile as well.

Cinnia recognized the girl's effort with an appreciative nod. "Well done. I need to speak with you as soon as you are done."

Cinnia gave Roark a glance to say she was done, but there would be more conversations.

Roark smiled at the departing princess, happy that a detente was established but still wary of how connected she might be to her father at her own admission. As she walked away, Roark looked over the horizon to find the owl that she knew was Cinnia's familiar. With all watchers accounted for, she opened the small stone and removed the message. In a quick glance she had her answer and a plan was starting to form. Now all she had to do was move all of the pieces into place.

"How are you, my love?" she asked the scout who stood beaming at having accomplished her solo mission.

"Singed in some places, but in fine form otherwise."

"Do I need to salve your burns, or will you live?"

"Ooh, tempting, but I fear it will have to wait if I know you."

"Yes, regrettably, it was just a hollow wish to be able to hold you for a moment. It will have to wait until we are on the other side of this challenge. Can you get them to the other side of this region alone? I wont be far off, but I need to get ahead of you to set up for our pursuers."

"I've been there once. I can get there again. You will be alone, what if we stay in contact. I can tell you what is happening in case we need to adjust."

"How do we connect?"

The girl smiled a childish grin and Roark knew what was to follow would be devious.

"You will want me to keep them focused on me. I need to draw them in, so I will. As we make the passes on each ridge, I'll make myself visible to them, so they remain interested in the bait, but I'll also give you a signal. Something simple so it looks unimportant, but lets you know if anything is wrong or changing."

Roark smiled at how well she understood what was happening. She wanted to hug her for it, and several other reasons, but they had to remain focused.

For the next few minutes they shared plans for how they would communicate across the peaks of the Spine and what would happen at the end of the journey ahead of them. By the time they were done, Roark knew they were as ready as they could be to descend into the dangers that lay ahead of them. The risk was that they would make a mistake and Cinnia's father would catch them before they reached their goal. It would be a balancing act. She would be trusting the skills of her scout, but she had little doubt in her scarlet fox.

As they separated for the final time until they both reached their target together, Roark felt the worry bubbling just below the surface. She pushed it down into the place she put everything she could do nothing about. She would worry about that later. Now was the time to act.

~~~

Reva was crossing another flat section of the ridge they had been climbing when Cinnia grabbed her arm and stopped her.

"What are you doing?"

"My Lady, what do you mean?"

"You know exactly what I mean, where are you taking us? Why are you keeping us out on this ridge? We're completely exposed out here. We ran fast and indirect to the West for two days, and now we pop up on every ridge like a flag." Her exasperation showed in her lack of control with the young scout.

"We're ahead of them, My Lady. We are not at risk here."

"That is not you speaking, child. You take the most indirect route to your own sleeping chambers. Tell me the truth."

Reva blushed as her leader called out her deception. She needed to keep this up for a little longer. Roark needed their followers to be drawn in completely before they broke. The stress of maintaining the just-enough pace for the past two days was wearing on her. She needed just a little longer. One more valley. They continued to follow. The wizard was afraid of the Guardian, or at least cautious. However, it was becoming clear that they were beginning to believe Roark had abandoned them. All the better. They would be more confident when they closed to take them in the next pass.

"If you would trust me, My Lady, this is to end this pursuit and give us a chance to survive."

"This is Roark's plan then?"

"Partly, I agreed with it. We developed it together."

"You trust her?"

"How can you ask that? She went back alone for Elsa and Alexa. She has saved us all more than once in this inhospitable land. You would be dead many times over where it not for her."

"I remind you, she only came back with one of them."

"You cannot blame her for that. You're lucky she brought back any." The accusation was carefully veiled, but present.

Cinnia flushed at the statement, then grudgingly nodded acceptance of the truth. Reva knew Alexa had haltingly shared what description she could of the events in the camp with the Princess. Even though

Reva had not heard it, Roark's eyes told her enough, and she knew of the King's tendencies.

"Can you tell me our goal at least?"

"Ahead of us, around this bend and over that valley beyond," she pointed ahead of them, "there is a pass. It is narrow and dangerous. We knew we could not stay ahead of them forever, so we decided to take advantage of our weakness."

"You're drawing them into an ambush?"

"Yes."

"Are you sure they're going to take the bait?"

"They have been for the past two days. They grow confident even now. Soon they will be convinced that they can overtake us safely, and we will let them."

"Where?"

"My Lady, please. If I show you, if they even think I know, they will become too cautious or too brave. Some time ahead, I will tell you they are following us, and we must run. When I say, we will run as fast as we can without losing them, which will not be hard. They have to think they have us panicked and pursue us into the pass without thinking. We must be the prey they expect."

"Why don't they just shoot us from this ridge?" she asked with her frustration again showing to her young maid.

"We're at a bad angle for that. They can see us, but not clearly enough to know if we're alone, and this is a more advantageous position for me as an archer."

Cinnia nodded and released Reva'a arm.

"Did I hurt our chances by asking?"

"No, they can't see us that clearly."

"What about the wizard?"

"My Lady, you are the expert there. You tell me."

She pointed into the sky at a speck that spiraled above them.

Reva knew that she blanched a little. If he saw them talking, it could make him suspicious. At least the raven was to far away to hear them.

"But you are following him as well aren't you?"

Cinnia stared at the scout as if she had told a secret to their enemy, then smiled.

"Yes. I've followed him since you joined us again. I've been left out of this plan."

"You understand why, don't you?"

"Roark doesn't trust me. I swore to her I would not get in her way."

"She doesn't trust your father. You are a pawn in all of this, and you know it now. She is not sure how much your father can see of what you see and know. She doesn't know what magic he may be using to back up his *bloodhounds*."

Cinnia nodded and waved away the concern. Reva knew she was sensible, but in this she was not being cautious enough. It had to hurt to be left out of the plans, but she had to realize why.

"Tell me anything you know. It may help."

"He cast a powerful scrying last night. As powerful as a wizard can produce. He was looking for something. I think it was Roark. He is nervous. He is not as confident as you think he is."

Reva nodded and pointed forward so they could move into the trees to obscure her father's view of them. Alexa followed quietly.

"Does he know where she is?"

"No, I don't think so. For some reason he was frustrated in his search."

Reva smiled. Roark was very skilled at staying hidden both physically and magically. She may not know the depth of her skills, but she did protect herself innately from magic and observation. It was a skill Reva respected.

"His spell from last night was powerful and it returned nothing. He conjured a gate and brought in another *bloodhound*."

"You think it's focused on her?"

"I'm afraid so."

"How? He has nothing to use?"

The Princess shrugged. They both knew it only took a hair to track with, and there had been several opportunities for her father to get what he needed. The spy in their camp earlier could have left him any number of markers.

"Can you not help?"

"I don't want to give away my own abilities to him. It is important that he remain unsure of the true powers of the enchantress sisterhood. Dara hurt us with her actions. They feared her already because of the tales from this cursed region, but now they have actual experience with her power. He will come harder now. Others will suffer."

"Forgive me, my Lady. I mean no disrespect, but do you want to die with your powers still locked in a dowry chest?"

The Princess blushed again and patted the young girl's cheek with true affection.

"You *are* the wise one my little fox. Lead us to this ambush. Where will Roark be?"

"She is ahead by now. Waiting in the pass. She will be on the western ridge."

Cinnia nodded and began kneading her hands together as she thought. Reva recognized the look and knew her mistress was devising a plan that would augment what Roark had already established. Reva glanced behind her and down as the rock that was blocking their view fell away for a moment.

In the brush and trees below, she could see the tell-tales of their pursuit. They had closed the gap spurred by some unknown new courage. If they didn't make the next wash ahead of them this would all be for nothing. Reva increased the pace and Cinnia noted the change with a click of the tongue.

She was now part of the plan. Wouldn't Roark be surprised. Reva grinned and wondered for a moment if that would be a good or bad thing.

GUARDIAN'S GAMBIT

Roark was feeling the effort that it Had taken to work her way above the others and then pass them while maintaining an eye on the pursuers. She needed to be careful to save energy for what was ahead.

After she had passed them, she had to rely on Reva's surreptitious signals and signs. That had been her idea, and Roark was glad she had offered it. She would not have been able to get as far ahead as she needed without the scout's help.

As she looked down the last wash that Reva had navigated and the brigands were now climbing, she felt a chill of expectation. She laid all of her arrows out in a row on the rock. She had her matched knives and her swords ready. It was the first time she was going into battle in her new form and she felt exhilarated to be facing this foe this way. She would never hide behind her old form again.

A flutter of movement above her drew her attention to the same raptor that had been circling her since she had found her perch. This was neither the Princess' owl nor her father's raven. So, this bird was someone else's who was interested in the outcome of this conflict. She rolled over and drew back a single arrow. She could never hit it, but she could scare whoever was controlling it.

As soon as she had the arrow back to her ear the bird fell from the sky like a stone. It fell as fast as her own arrow would have flown and before she could even move the bird had closed the distance. In a flutter of wings, it settled beside her on the flat stone where her arrows were arrayed. Roark stared at it. She had no idea what a wizard could do with a familiar like this falcon. She didn't know what power might be facing her.

The falcon stepped back and forth on its claws and pushed its head back and forth at Roark. It wanted something, but what.

As Roark watched it dance about, it opened its beak and dropped a small gem onto the stone.

Roark hesitated.

She didn't know this bird.

Where had it come from?

It was obvious it was being controlled, but by whom.

What harm could a stone do to her? Her skin tingled with fear at what magic could be held in that stone. Maybe it was a message stone like the spy had used.

The bird squawked and shifted on its claws.

Roark cautiously reached out and picked up the stone.

She looked at it. It was a small ruby and it had no breaks or signs of an opening. The bird seemed appeased and waited. The ladies were now running toward her and their pursuers would be close on their heals if they were running. She didn't have time to figure out what the bird wanted. She closed her fist on the small gem in frustration.

Her vision exploded in color and detail she was not used to. She was glad she was laying down because she was no longer looking at the bird. She was instead looking at herself and the disorientation would have made her fall down.

With a squawk of satisfaction, the bird leapt into the air and Roark experienced a sudden lurch in her gut as she rode with the bird. She could see the whole valley and the wash. She could see the men clearly climbing up it in a hurry. Several stumbled and dislodged large stones to tumble away and endanger their companions. All the wizard needed was for one of them to make the top and capture the fleeing trio.

Two of the men exposed themselves to take advantage of a straight section. Roark watched as Reva's bow taught them not to get too cocky. Each man fell back into the dry wash with an arrow sunk through their necks up to the fletching.

The Falcon's vision showed the spray of blood that blew back on the men behind them as the bladed points cut the artery in each man's neck. That was when she saw it. The bumbling brute of a *bloodhound* stumbled over the edge of the pass. His dazed and stupid eyes were fixed on the area of the Princess and Alexa and he grinned with satisfaction that he had them so near. His whole body seemed to shiver with the excitement of knowing where they were.

Someone had released it from its chains.

It was free to hunt for what it lusted after. Roark knew nothing would stop the animal once it caught its prey.

She released the grip on the gem and her vision returned to her with an uncomfortable snap of reality in her mind. She turned back to look over her place on the ridge, blinking to clear the pain.

Reva was now running as if she had hoped her shots would keep them from chasing. The men in the wash did not take the attack as a warning but as a challenge. A woman had killed two of their number. She would pay for that.

Roark calculated the time it would take for those men to climb up out of the wash and reach the top. Reva's attack had been perfect. They were not going to stop until they had the women, and Reva was telling Cinnia where to run so that the ambush could succeed.

Reva had worked the men up into a frenzy. It was apparent they really believed Roark had abandoned the Princess to her own devices and that was all the better.

Roark waited. If she started shooting too soon, before they were fully in the pass, they would just retreat. She took that short moment to check the count against what Reva had told her was following. Maybe she would find the wizard. She saw the commander of the men chasing them. She saw the twenty soldiers she had counted earlier, but she didn't see the wizard. That worried her. She hated having an unaccounted-for piece off the board where she couldn't see it. She knew he was a coward who engaged from a distance and retreated to safety, but to not even close when the women he had sent to die in the Spine were alone and defenseless surprised her. She grabbed the gem again and hoped the bird might understand her need. She didn't have a lot of time to find him.

Her eyes blurred again and burned, but then she could see the valley again. The men were breaking over the top and running after Cinnia and Alexa led by the lumbering beast which salivated at the nearness of his prey. Reva was raising up to prepare a shot. Roark had time. She focused on what she wanted, and the falcon climbed higher. She needed to know where the wizard King was.

In a couple of climbing circles, she found him. He was in a small cluster of trees at the base of the last wash with a band of six men. He was focused on something. It was clear in the eyes of the falcon that he was chanting and motioning with his hands. Roark did not want to know what the man was calling down on them. She didn't want to give him time to finish his enchantment, but she couldn't stop him this far out.

Roark released the gemstone and returned to the pass below her. Reva had taken out two more but had been forced to evade up higher into the rocks. A pair were chasing her, and the brute was struggling to remove an arrow from his arm. He was crying in pain and frustration at being thwarted. Either she had planned the shot because she knew something Roark didn't or she had been rushed. Roark didn't take time to figure it out. She wasn't sure if Reva was still holding back or she was really pressed.

The others had stopped chasing and were forming two cautious ranks. They were almost committed to the pass now. A mousy looking man, not the commander and not one of the soldiers, was holding back at the top of the wash. He wasn't following. All he was doing was watching. Roark made a bet that he was the wizard's man. He was what the spell was about.

Roark nocked an arrow released it and followed it with her second shot as she thought about the man at the top of the wash. Her two arrows struck home in the backs of the two men harassing Reva. She was quick and getting away, but Roark needed her bow. She could not shoot while running.

With Reva clear to fight again, Roark returned her attention to the man at the wash. He was holding something and staring. He was not moving. It was a long range shot but Roark felt it was a critical one to take. This had something to do with the wizard.

She drew back the bow and arched her shot up to reach the mousy one. With a little calculation she dropped her aim slightly and then released the arrow to the fates. In the periphery of her vision she could see the commander in the pass pointing toward her. They had found her. They knew it was an ambush, but they were not sure who she was, she had dropped her male persona and they had only seen her as the Guardian.

She pivoted while drawing her next arrow back and releasing one directly into the chest of the commander. Reva dropped two more in the same cluster and the men suddenly realized they had two attackers and this was not the easy rout they had expected. A set of archers were releasing arrows toward Reva, but she was already scampering away from her last position. Roark wanted to be proud, but they were running out of time and arrows. She quickly checked that Cinnia and Alexa were safely on the other side of the pass but not beyond. Roark Released another two arrows into the archers reducing the number of men who were actively trying to kill them by two more.

She counted her arrows carefully. Two more, as she expected. She also counted the men. Around ten remained. There was no way they could kill them all with arrows. Reva had more, by choice, so in two more shots Roark would have to surrender the safety of her perch and take the fight to the men directly. She stole a moment as Reva released another arrow at the archers to check on the wizard. What she saw told her it was time to end this ambush and move on.

She released the stone and placed it in a pouch on her belt. The *bloodhound* had recovered from the failed shot from Reva. It was a single-minded beast that was frustrated when distracted and angered easily. It demonstrated that frustration and anger as it turned back toward the two women who had its attention. Cinnia and Alexa shifted away from the beast and it followed. Roark had killed the last one with a dagger to the back of the neck, but there was no way she could be that accurate from here. Not with her bow.

She fired her last two arrows with rapid succession. She had aimed for the spine and heart of the beast with no idea which direction it would move. The first arrow pierced its back just to the right of the spine and struck the shoulder blade. The second hit just below the first and pierced the beast's lung.

A howl that started with the first arrow continued with a froth of blood that showered from the *bloodhound's* mouth. It looked back and up at Roark with anger in its eyes as it reached back to try and get at the pain in its shoulder. It spun around a few times trying to release the arrows before it grunted a bloody grunt and turned back to face the women it wanted.

Roark couldn't allow this to fall apart because of the wizard's beast. She drew her sword and knife in her classic form and started her descent to face the force she had stopped in the pass.

The beast stumbled forward in painful steps trying to figure out what was hurting it.

With a roar she had learned defending the caravans, she threw herself over the edge. Her transformation, which had felt odd most of her life, now comforted her. She knew her armored hide gave her an advantage. She looked down at her taloned hands and arms which bristled with draconic spines and grinned as her roar drew the attention of the men below. This was the legend that preceded her. This was what those men feared, and it was coming for them. It had no effect on the beast chasing Cinnia, but it was holding back the men who knew fear.

She leapt from stone landing to stone outcropping as she raced down to meet them. She continued to roar her assault cry knowing that she was the only attacker. They would be prepared to face her. If she was foolish and too brave, she would probably die at their feet. That was not the plan for today. If she died, Cinnia and Alexa would never get away. Reva knew her duty as soon as Roark engaged them directly, use her last arrows to kill all she could and then disengage.

"Don't look back once you walk away. Get them away." Were Roark's last instructions as she wiped the plan back into the earth.

Roark felt rather than saw the arrows thud into the front two attackers who stood somewhat flat footed at her approach.

The farthest men out from her were breaking and running back toward the safety of the wash they had just climbed up. The legend and her form was working.

Roark had not cut off their retreat. The closest, a cluster of about five men, had drawn swords and were preparing to meet her, but she needed to deal with the *bloodhound* first.

Sudden movement at her side surprised her. There should not be any enemy coming from that quarter so she felt sure she was safe from attack, but it was distracting her. A shimmering disk of air swirled next to her and Alexa stepped from the center of it equipped with a sword— apparently freed from a dead man's body— drawn and wearing a grim battle mask.

Roark grinned as she realized Reva may have altered the plan somewhat. It was a risk, but she knew it was how they lived. They had sworn to protect the Princess with their lives. Alexa's normally soft features were contorted with her mask of hate and concentration. Roark sent a prayer to several deities for the woman beside her who was throwing herself at the very beast that had tortured her. She didn't raise any prayers for the creature or the men who created it. They deserved what came for them.

As they reached the front-line defenders Roark parried the first strike at her as Alexa's sword struck at the *bloodhound*. It blocked her strikes with meaty arms that felt no pain as her blade sliced them.

It tried to grab her. Her recovery was quick and brutal slices to its torso.

Roark released Alexa to the fates and thrust her own dirk up under the rib of the man she had parried. She had no time to devote to keeping up with the others. She threw the limp body leaning on her arm into the back of the beast to help Alexa and turned to face the next man. He paused.

She propelled herself into an attack striking the man's blade. He suddenly realized he could die and fought back. She parried and then struck with her fighting knife. The man dropped his sword as her blade found meat in his forearm. She spun around using the momentum of her attack to bring her sword around in a continuation of her first attack. It cut into the man's throat and he fell away from the attack spurting his life into the air. Roark continued to cross behind the *bloodhound* who continued to lunge at Alexa. The woman seemed to be tempting him forward to his death one step and slice at a time. That was a dangerous game to play in a running fight. Too many others had ideas of how it should end.

With efficient strikes Roark dispatched two more men who were edging toward Alexa and aiming to help the brute.

The front rank had fallen, and the rest were running away. As the din of the battle settled and Roark's hearing returned to her she heard the flat smack of metal against flesh. She turned slightly, not sacrificing her defense to see Alexa spin away after smashing the flat of her sword blade across the dumb, shocked face of the *bloodhound*. In her periphery she watched the other men run toward the wash and the safety of their wizard leader. Satisfied they were safe she pivoted and drove her sword through the beast's back, severing his spine and piercing his heart. Her blade thrust through his chest with a spray of blood that showered Alexa and brought her somewhat out of her reverie. She looked at Roark with a slight glimmer of anger. The girl had been enjoying playing with the animal. With a final exhale, it fell forward onto its knees and slipped off of Roark's sword.

Reva stepped out with her last arrows nocked and aimed at the backs of the retreating force. Her chest was heaving from the exertion. She relaxed her draw and let them run. Her arrow would probably not find a target if she had released it.

Roark looked around. Cinnia had held her position where Reva had told her to. Alexa beamed with her own recovery. Her right hand was mindlessly plunging her sword into the body of the dead *bloodhound*.

Roark pulled the small gem from her pouch and gripped it to join the bird circling above the retreating men.

Few of them actually made it to the bottom of the wash without injury and many of them would not recover from their injuries. The wizard, who had lost his eyes on the attack, and subsequently the focus of his spell, was standing at the side of the wash watching as his brigands, those who survived, ran past him as if they were still being chased.

Roark released her grip on the gem to reach over and take Reva's bow. It was a long shot, but she wanted to take it.

She nocked an arrow, drew back the composite bow, and aimed at a place in the air that would give her the best arc. With a patient control of her breath she aligned the bow on the markers she remembered from the falcon's vision and released. It was a long shot. She wanted to send a message. She wanted him shaken.

The arrow streaked away from her bow and she held it long enough to guarantee that it flew true. Then she returned the bow and again took the gem out and gripped it.

The falcon was still circling the wizard and he was staring at the bird with understanding in his eyes. The bird did not look at the arrow but continued to hold the attention of the wizard. Roark could only hope that it was on target when the wizard reacted by raising his hand and shouting a command. Nothing happened that Roark could see but the arrow that was on target slammed into an invisible barrier that seemed to extend from the wizard's hand. The shaft shattered from the force generated by the terminal velocity fall toward the target. The wizard waited a moment to drop his shield and then pointed toward the west where the falcon could see him.

Roark understood the meaning of that sign and the arrogance of the man who had sent it.

"Be ready!" Roark shouted.

~ ~ ~

Roark directed the falcon toward the west and scanned the forest for the signs she knew would be there. Quickly she made out the movement. They were coming. Reinforcements were on their way and soon they would be in trouble. The wizard had almost arranged to ambush the ambushers.

Reva looked at her and started collecting arrows from the dead, both those in their quivers and those in their bodies. Even the damaged shafts that were not too bad would injure. With an overfull quiver and a nod, she ran toward the pass and vanished into the brush. Even watching her, Roark was not sure where she went. It was as if the forest itself had swallowed her and hidden all signs of her passing.

For a moment stolen from their shared plan, Roark watched after Reva. She focused on where she had been and thought of her own magic. Wisps of magical energy still hung in the air and Roark could see them. They were dissipating even as she watched for them. Reva had passed through the undergrowth cleanly and as she had, she had changed form.

Was Reva really the legendary goddess she seemed to be? Why was she hiding with this band of mortals if she was? Roark had more to think about at the moment, but the beautiful vixen captivated her in that instant.

Roark shook off the charm and turned her attention back to the plan. For this to work she had to be in the right place as the brigands broke free from the forest and saw clear light ahead of them to make the pass. She collected a quiver, bow, and arrows from the dead as she prepared the pass. Alexa silently cleaned her blade on the brute's body and started collecting gear as well. She pulled a bow from a dead hand and took his quiver.

Roark turned to face Cinnia.

"A fight is coming. Be prepared to hold this pass if any make it past us. I don't want your father to see any of his men break over that side."

Cinnia winked at her. Roark left them holding the pass.

She walked out to the point where she would be just slightly above and to the left flank of the approaching column coming from the West.

She watched as the head of the group broke through the brush into an opening. The first head to break through was familiar. His round facial features and the glazed distant stare told her that he was simple. The way he sniffed at the air like a hound drew her attention. He paused and looked around. First he looked toward her, and then in the direction that Reva was moving. In each direction he took a deep inhale and then several quick inhales through his nose. It was hard to ignore the similarities to a hound. They had another *bloodhound*. The beast stopped and stood still in the middle of the small square of clear space. His large muscular chest heaved as he sampled the air around him. The fat of his cheeks seemed to hang around his rounded face and his ears did not seem to stand up but to droop. His armor showed signs of rust and lack of care as did the brute's clothes. He carried a hammer and an axe in each hand that he used to cut and pound at his surroundings. His confused eyes belied the truth. He shifted his weight forward and thrust his whole body toward Roark. The lust and hunger in its face caused a shiver of anxiety to race up Roark's spine. She was a dragon, but that magic beast wanted her.

The arrow was free from the quiver and on the string almost before she thought to draw it. Roark was staring at the correct arch to reach the golem. She marked her spot, drew the bow the last few inches, relaxed, released the breath, and, as she settled herself into the release, she felt the string roll from her fingers with a snap. The first arrow was away as she pulled the second and released it on a similar but slightly altered path.

She adjusted the aim again and released the third arrow before she would have to reposition. She knew it was an alteration to their plan, but she didn't expect the *bloodhound*.

The first arrow fell upon its victim silently. It would have slammed through the protective chain links in the mail shirt the brute wore, except the *bloodhound* had brought its hammer up in time to defend itself. There was something else in this one. Some magic intelligence was at work.

The second and third arrows were on their way and this time the beast didn't defend. Roark relaxed. These would kill it. She could move on with the plan.

The first struck and shattered without piercing the flesh. The bodkin point, designed to pierce armor, did nothing. The final arrow failed as well and the vile beast stepped forward toward her with a lascivious grin on its face.

She had no choice now. She had to face it.

Focusing on keeping Reva safe and able to continue her attack, Roark rushed to face him.

Roark could feel her own pulse racing as she ran into the attack. She allowed her own magic to bolster her protection. She was going to need it. This beast was a proxy and she had to take it down. On the run she stowed her bow and focused on her natural weapons. She let her arms grow stronger and her body to take on more of her dragon form. Her legs became stronger and she sped toward the fight. She knew the men were closing around them as she reached the clearing where the *bloodhound* stood panting for her.

She didn't stop. Her first strike cut across the torso and chain mail of the brute.

Her black talons raked the rings. Blue sparks flew away from each claw as she also ripped the magical shield away from the beast.

It reached both arms out to grab her, but she couldn't allow it. She jumped up with her left leg and thrust her right leg out to dig claws into its chest.

Metal rings surrendered as rivets split. Blood streamed from the deep wounds she left behind as she flipped away from the grasping brute.

Somehow, he grabbed her right foot and stopped her escape. Instead of a graceful flip to safety, he slammed her roughly into the ground. She felt the rock and dirt spew away as she landed hard.

She rolled away and kicked at him to avoid getting trapped by the beast, then quickly jumped into the air. She found the line of men closing on her but could do nothing to stop them. If they trapped her she could be in trouble.

She landed on all fours. Her body had changed as her fear caused her to need more protection. Her neck and head were fully reptilian. Her spine was ridged, and she could feel the tail she had recently felt for the first time swish at the air.

The *bloodhound* was not sure where to grab at her long body. He wanted to catch her more now. His eyes shimmered like a small boy staring at a lizard he wanted to catch.

She whipped her tail around and smacked him hard in the face. Blood spewed from his lip where her scales and the force of the hit ruptured it. With a quick reversal, she slapped him again. This time the spines on her tail cut a gash from his ear to his chin. The bone of his jaw showed white.

He was stunned.

She took advantage before the men surrounded her and grabbed his right arm. Surprise filled his stunned eyes. With her right claw she grabbed his head. The talons closed over the thick skull and dug into the meat. Blood welled up at each penetration. With a twist like she was removing a cork from a bottle, she snapped the neck. Resistance stopped. The eyes clouded and dilated. She released his head. With nothing left supporting him, his body fell from her grasp and slumped to the floor of the clearing.

As quickly as the fight had started it was over. She could feel the sand falling from the glass. She was not sure how her fight had changed Reva's plan. She could only hope was in place. Learning from the fox, she drew on her own magic and slipped into the cover of the forest making her passage as silent as she could.

Her attack had drawn the column forward to surround what seemed like the line of attack. With quick repositioning she was now fully on their left flank. She was not sure how wide they were spread out, so she could already be inside their line, but she had not heard any sign of them rapidly deploying around her. She paused on a slight rise next to a vine covered tree to catch her breath and listen to the forest.

The brigands were not being quiet as they rushed to meet her assault. It had been mere seconds for her to reach this point. From what she could hear, she was drawing a picture in her mind of their formation. It looked like they were still trying to block the pass and surround her where she had been.

She reformed into her human shape again and clutched the stone. The falcon's vision told her that she was right. She had penetrated their line. Time to take advantage of it. She slipped her bow off of her back and nocked another arrow, after slipping the stone back in her pouch.

With time to think, she paid attention to the steps she took. As if in slow motion, she felt the rounded nock point on the sinew string between her fingers as she checked it. In her mind, she chanted a childhood rhyme about the feline's guts that had made it and asked the beast's ghost to vitalize it, it took but a moment and was mostly in her mind. She felt the tingle pass through her and into the string.

As her hand reached the arrow, she called to the turkey's spirit to aid the arrows flight, and the forest to strengthen the spine of the arrow. Again, she listened to her magic fill the arrow. Her actions she had taken since she had started fighting as a Guardian, since she had become Roark, made sense to her. The little actions were simply her explanations for the magic she now knew she controlled.

By the time she had the arrows nocked and the bow drawn back to her ear, she knew the powers she had infused into her attack. With her mind she called on her form to quicken her muscles and focus her aim. With the final release of her breath she released the string and the arrow raced toward her selected target.

The world snapped back to real time as she progressed to aim and release three more enchanted arrows before she returned her bow to her back and abandoned her rise and protective tree.

Ahead of her, the line that was trying to trap them crumbled as they realized they were under attack. Roark was already running toward her next point of attack and listening to determine if she needed to disengage or press the attack. The noise of battle as the brigands began to react to the attack from their middle, on two sides, encouraged her that there was hope that they could hold or even push back this force, but that was not the last surprise coming for these men from Parthia.

She could feel the forest beneath her as she ran, her thighs and shoulders burned with the effort. The scales along her shoulders and back trembled in the breeze, sensing the movement around her and warning her of where her attackers were moving.

Roark was more aware of her own self in this fight than she ever had been. She was realizing things she had never paid any attention to. In the past she had just fought to survive and never realized what was happening. Cinnia and Reva had helped her see and understand what she had been doing all along, and Roark was learning in the moment how to maximize her abilities.

As she leapt across a wide chasm in the defile that fell away from the pass to surmount a high point of black rock jutting from the ground, she grabbed the rough edge and pulled herself up onto the top. As she stood up, she turned full circle on the precipice to see what was below her. The height advantage was only a few feet, but it gave her the view she needed.

The brigands were falling back in ragged clumps. Smaller pockets to the right, cut off by Reva's attack were retreating toward that center to create a protective box. She did not want them to make it.

Her fingers touched the arrows she had remaining to give her a quick inventory. She did not want to engage them close up, not yet. They were still too strong.

With her mind focused on the field ahead of her, she selected her last targets. It was the cut off group closest to the gap and Cinnia. There were ten brigands working as a team to shield each other. She waited for the moment when the advantage she had was just right and then rapidly poured her last arrows into the group. It was not a haphazard attack, however. She focused each arrow on a weak point hoping to stop them where they were. If it succeeded, then she could focus on the central box of the advancing force and wipe it out. With help, she could pass through their lines one more time in a close-range attack. She might even be able to break them. The were a small force. Enough to take three women and a single Guardian, surely. Roark smiled.

She listened for the signs that Reva was engaged on the other flank. Her ears twitched in the light breeze and sampled both the sounds and any movement near her. Her thighs twitched, and she leapt from her precipice to the floor of the defile. Her front claws gripped the firm soil. They dug in for a moment to increase her speed toward the central cluster of brigands. Her heart pounded in her chest as she raced toward the conflict.

To her right she could sense more than hear Reva harrying them with her own attacks. She could smell the fear and anger on the air as she approached the wall of men. Swords thrust out at her as she raced at them.

She didn't even think about each weapon as she dipped her shoulder under one and rolled her body around another. Her eyes were focused on how to damage them as she rushed past them.

As her left shoulder rolled away from the thrust of a sword, she reached out with her fore claws and raked them across an exposed thigh. The chain mail of her target had fallen away as he tried to impale her on his sword, so she had no problem ripping four long gashes down and along the inner thigh of his right leg. He screamed as she ripped fabric and flesh. Blood spurted out of the deep cuts, but she didn't pause. The other men were still trying to kill her.

She pushed off of the attackers left side as her rear claws landed on him, dug in to whatever she could grab, and thrust away. He was a weak foundation for her, so she was slowed in her next move. She could not attack again and was forced to drive her shoulder into her next attacker's groin as she continued across the left side of the protective box of soldiers. The spiked ridge did some damage and he fell aside.

Roark's nose twitched as her angled cheeks pulled back from her long elongate eye teeth. Out of the corner of her eye she saw a spearman reach over the top of the protecting wall. The point harried her approach. A red blur landed on his shoulder and his spear fell from distracted hands. The blur turned more distinct as it stopped, perched on his shoulder for a moment.

Roark wanted to watch, but the brigand she had knocked off balance was recovering and stabbing a sword at her chest. Her forward movement had been arrested and the other brigands were reacting to her threat more than Reva as she raked the pikeman and jumped from head to head across the brigands still trying to stab Roark.

Roark bit down on the sword hand of her attacker and pushed away from the sword thrust at her side. The tip clipped her along the scales at her ribs, but the trust was arrested and losing strength as she dug her teeth into the soft skin of his wrist. She could feel the muscles relax and the sword fall away as her fangs broke through the leather and metal of his gauntlet and the skin beneath. Blood filled her mouth in a hot stream and her attacker screamed and yanked hard to recover his arm.

His violent jerk dug her teeth into him deeper. She needed to get away, so she bit down and pulled away. The artery, exposed as his arm severed, spewed blood across her cheek and down her side as she pushed off of the ground again with all four limbs.

Reva bounced off of the shoulder of the brigand who was paying more attention to his thigh wound to land beyond the reach of the brigands on Roark's left side and scampered away into the undergrowth.

Roark's larger mass took longer to accelerate from a stop, but in a moment she was following the red blur into the same cover. She kept the red and white image of Reva's tail ahead of her as she gained on the small fox. In a few strides, Roark had caught up with her and was running beside her through the undergrowth. Although she really wanted to take a moment to gamble about with Reva, she remained focused on the attacking force.

They had split the brigand force. More than half of the vanguard were dead from their arrows or their strike. Fifteen men clustered into a phalanx trying to protect themselves from a beast they had not come to face. Noise beyond the front rank promised reinforcements were closing on them and would be supporting the cluster of men soon. She knew the bloodied men would not stop now. Once the force behind them closed, they would push into the pass.

Roark could not stop them, there were too many to stop with just the three of them. The Wizard had them and would soon be closing the trap he had set.

Without a sound they both slowed their run to a slow canter. They were far enough away that they were safe from the men.

Reva's form started to shift before Roark. Her long thin muzzle started to draw up into her face. Her body expanded from the small form in a smooth graceful flow.

With a thought she triggered her own transformation. It was quick and painless.

Roark reached out to wrap Reva in her arms. The woman's softness and warmth snuggled into her chest. Her face nuzzled into Roark's neck, enfolding her in a calm, knowing embrace.

Reva looked up into her eyes and spoke for the first time since they had joined the battle.

"Is everything ready?"

"I think it is. Let's see if he's been watching."

~~~

The falcon flew in a circle over the pass. Cinnia rested against the wall on the western side watching for a sign that the Parthian forces had been routed and she could head toward the border and her safety. Alexa stood with her sword drawn ready to defend her Lady.

The bird shifted its direction and looked into the forest leading to the Parthian border. Movement, another twenty men, closed on the cluster that Roark and Reva had stopped outside of the gap.

In a diving turn the bird crossed the pass to the east and found the remnant of the Wizard's forces. They were rallying at the bottom of the wash that led up to the ambush point Roark had used to push them back.

From above, it was clear that Cinnia was trapped and would never reach Parthia. All of their efforts were for nothing and the two sides of this wizard's plot were about to meet and close out this pursuit in the Dragon's Spine.

In another circle above the pass the falcon showed that both sides were now moving forward. The wizard knew his forces were still strong and had the advantage. The Parthian forces were moving toward the pass again stopping any advance. The wizard's last men, a handful that were approaching the pass with him were closing any retreat.

Roark released the stone and her vision returned to the face of the worried scout.

"Both sides are advancing to close the gap."

Reva smiled her most childlike smile and Roark was reminded of how dangerous she was. It was like looking at the keen edge of a knife as it was poised to slice into its target.

"Go, and be safe," Roark said to her as she looked to the west.

"You as well, we shall meet soon." Her smile became a determined grin and she shifted into her fox form as she bolted into the brush.

Roark focused her own thoughts and transformed again. She was thinking of the speed she would need to make her way to the spot she wanted, and she felt her body meet that form.

She stretched out into her snake like form. Her strong rear legs thickened and propelled her into the climb up the walls of the ridge. In long bounds she leapt up to the peak that looked down on both forces closing toward the center.

When she reached the top and could see as well as the falcon, she withdrew the stone and checked again on the wizard. His force was climbing up the wash and were almost to the top. Soon they would be committed to the pass.

She checked on Reva and saw her atop the crest to the west flashing the signal on her side. Roark gave the falcon a final thought and released it. She then flashed a similar signal to the east and waited above the pass to watch.

The wizard King stepped over the edge of the pass and stood up to look at his victory. Roark could see down into the pass clearly. The Parthian soldiers had broken through the forest edge and were now walking like a wall toward the pass to close off any chance Cinna had to escape.

Roark looked to the small rise where Reva had been and noted that she was gone. The falcon had landed next to Cinnia. To the east Roark could see that a force of Guardians, supported by occupants of the pass were closing any retreat behind the Wizard. Roark checked him. His confidence was clearly leading his actions now. He was standing with his hands on his hips and a wand loosely in his left hand.

Roark focused a moment and felt the tingle as she obscured herself with a coloration that matched the stone around her. Then she focused on what she could hear and see.

"Cinnia, daughter, you have made this far too difficult."

Cinnia looked terrified as she stepped from behind her lady-in-waiting. She stood erect, straightened her clothes, and reset her face to show defiance.

"It is your deception that has made this hard. You could have killed me in Arandor and saved yourself all of this trouble."

"Yes." His admission hit her hard and caused a momentary flash in her resolve. "But, having you killed in this horrible place while valiantly fighting for your life would have been so much better for me."

Roark felt the callousness in his words and knew they must be hammering Cinnia who had still hoped he was following orders from the other wizards.

"Surrender to these men and let them do what they came to do. I will make sure you are seen as a hero in the land for your efforts. You will not be forgotten."

Cinnia laughed at her father. The power behind the laugh seemed to cause him to lose an inch or two and he actually looked around at his men. Their faces showed fear. Roark had not been affected by it, but apparently there had been some magic in her laugh.

Roark looked west to check progress and noted that while they had been focused on the conversation in the pass several things had happened.

A raven lay in the dirt in front of a snow-white owl just ahead of the approaching Parthians. That force had been replaced by a larger force of Guardians. According to the plan, they had crept up behind them and quietly removed them. Roark could not see the Parthians anymore. She was sure they were no longer a threat and she really didn't care how that was true.

"You will not reach him," Cinna said as her father seemed to falter a little in his stance.

"Your raven. That twinge of pain you just felt, that was his death," Cinnia said defiantly drawing Roark's eyes back to the pass and the small cluster of men the wizard still commanded. Ten Guardians were crawling up behind the wizard who was searching the sky with a concerned look on his face.

A white streak flew low through the pass. As it climbed toward the sky, it dropped the limp body of the wizard's raven onto the ground.

The dead bird flopped onto the dirt and bounced once in a cloud of dust.

"Don't test me father. You've faced the power of an enchantress once. Do you want to taste more?"

Roark watched the wizard closely. He could not cast a spell exposed like he was. If he spoke the first word his death would be quick, and he had to know that.

He was starting to look around.

It was dawning on him that his position of power was turning into a trap.

He looked behind him and shouted an immediate warning.

His men turned to attack the approaching Force.

Arrows snapped away from drawn bows and thudded into the Wizard's final troops. Each fell into a heap without a sound.

The wizard's hand was raising the wand and Roark leapt from her perch. Her wings extended to slow her fall, but she needed to get down fast, so she dove directly at him.

She struck as his wand was leveling on Cinnia and his mouth was forming a power word.

Her claw raked his arm forcing his concentration to waver. The word turned into a howl of pain and the wand flew from his now weakened hand. It struck the wall of the pass and clattered across the rock as it flew out of his control.

Roark extended her wings and landed on the wizard with her rear legs. The wizard's breath left him as he landed on the ground beneath her claws.

The Guardians closed the gap on the eastern side stopping any chance that the wizard had of running. Cinnia picked up the wand and held it confidently pointed at her father's chest.

Roark stepped off of the trapped wizard and allowed her color to return to her natural red and black. Her forearms crossed her imposing chest and her serpentine neck bent to allow her dragon face to hover just above the wizard's.

Her wings were arched above her. She felt more powerful than she ever had and wanted this wizard to know who she was.

"You came here to do evil little wizard. I am the guardian of this region and I am here to exact justice. You will pay for your actions here."

Fear crossed the man's face as he fumbled to stand before her. She chose not to let him and bumped him with her chin causing him to sprawl in the dirt again.

"You have, however, been granted a stay of your sentence."

Roark looked back at Cinnia and then back at the wizard.

"Your daughter, a far better person than you, has asked that I spare you, for a year, to give you a chance to prove you are worth saving. Do not waste this one chance."

Roark twisted her neck and head again to look at Cinnia to see if she still wanted her to hold her vengeance. As her right eye took in the Princess,she could still see the wizard moving to reach something in his robe.

Roark felt the excitement build but allowed him to almost reach it. She wanted him to continue to believe he was as powerful as he believed. In the final instant, before his hand reached his robe and slipped in, Roark reacted and pinned him to the ground with her forearm and claw.

She left her forefinger claw lose and pointed it directly into the wizard's face.

"Do not press me and force me to go back on my word," she growled.

Her flaring nostrils were just above his chin and her forked tongue flicked out below it to further clarify that he was dealing with a real dragon.

He shuddered beneath her grip and nodded acquiescence. She released his arm and upper body slowly allowing him to withdraw his hand first.

She kept her claw close to him to reinforce her control until others arrived to disarm him. Reva slipped up quietly beneath her wings and next to her shoulder to let her know that all was clear with a nod.

"Wizard, your forces have been cleared all the way to the border and we will be taking you with us on this journey. I apologize that it will probably not be in the style you are accustomed to."

Roark nodded to the young scout. "Please disarm this man and tie him so that he has no use of his arms."

She adjusted her attention back to him and gave him a querying look.

"Do I need to gag you as well, or will you keep your magic tongue to yourself?"

The wizard croaked out a short response, "No gag is required." He swallowed his gorge and tried again to strengthen his voice. "I am the King of Arandor, you cannot hold me this way."

"Do not," she growled, "try to threaten me King. I am not afraid of your threat and you have invaded my land. Do so again and I will turn your land into cinders beneath you."

Roark was not sure she could do what she promised. She had just figured out how to take her full form, but she would do her best to live up to her promise if he continued.

The king ducked his head to her threat, and she knew she had him.

"If you start to act as a king, I may treat you like one," she said as she pulled away from him and let the others deal with him. Alexa drew the cords around his hands and arms with a pleasurable grin. She whispered something into his ear as she yanked the knot tight and the man's face blanched.

Roark wondered what she had told a wizard that had made him react so. She would have to ask Reva later to find out. It had to be a powerful threat for sure.

As she walked away from the wizard who was fully under control now, she transformed into her new Guardian form.

"I have done as I promised Lady Cinnia. He has a year to prove himself worthy. Rest and gather what we need. Tomorrow we will finish this caravan and I will fulfill this contract."

The Princess smiled at her and gave her a gracious curtsy before Roark turned to the west to meet up with her First. He needed to be complimented on his timing and planning.

GUARDIAN'S END GAME

Roark joined the Guardians closing on the pass from the east. Malich was leading a group of men who were carefully watching for any of the stragglers who may have fallen back from the wizard's approach. Their steps reminded her of how well trained they were. Always on guard and cautious of what may happen, she was sure none of the wizard's men would escape their net.

Malich looked forward after scanning the group and smiled at his approaching leader.

"Where 'ave ya been, boss?"

Roark felt relief flood her. Malich was her closest friend in the passes and had stood with her since they had joined the band to protect caravans. She had not realized how worried she was that he would not accept her without her makeup and facade. She smiled back at her second in command.

"I got caught up in a political problem and couldn't make the meetup. How did we do on the last caravan?"

"No good. We 'ad to let 'er go. Spies an' brigands in the weeds."

Roark crossed the gap between them in a couple of steps and embraced her friend. She was happy to see him alive and well.

He returned the embrace in a very cautious way and Roark realized she was embarrassing him. She separated and put out her hand. They clasped arms in the more formal meeting of Guardians.

The other men continued to watch for targets in a conspicuous attempt to not watch their leaders.

"You have good soldiers in that group Malich. You should be proud of your Guardians."

Malich stood straight up and looked her directly in the eyes.

"These're your men, boss. I'm 'ere as your First."

Roark looked at him for a moment and considered what he said. She knew that the truth about her had to have made it to her men, and she was not sure how they were going to accept it.

"Ya ha' ta know, they knew ya was odd 'afore any a this went on. We all stood wit' ya in the fight. We's all seen ya in tha' other form."

"And you kept this from me all this time? You let me keep up the mask?"

"It was best for the men and dealin' wit' the travelers."

Roark felt a relief she had not expected. Somewhere in the back of her mind she had worried about the loss of her position and her friends.

"Well then, get these prisoners rounded up. I want a strong guard on that wizard." She pointed into the gap at the cluster of women who had secured Cinnia's father.

"Get us to the border. Did you get the message through?"

"I sen' it. Best I can do."

Roark allowed that. Once someone from the Dragon's Spine entered another realm, it was up to the soldiers there how they handled them. She hoped that the message they carried had helped.

As they entered the pass, Malich took charge of the prisoner and assigned Guardians to protect the Princess and her remaining ladies. Roark walked on through the pass and toward the other group of her men who held the border.

They were all going about their normal duties. A camp was already forming where they could deal with injuries and prisoners. The recruits were gathering weapons, gear, and pouches from the dead and moving their bodies away from the camp. A beir was already being set up for later.

Roark was impressed by how her forces were handling themselves. As she approached the first group of recruits, they paused and saluted. She returned their respect and felt the pride of being herself among them. She had always feared being exposed, but now she realized they had known more than she had ever thought.

She passed through her lines and approached the border of the Spine. She knew where it was. She had crossed it many times to deliver other special cargo, but never to anyone of the rank she expected to greet there at sunrise.

She felt someone behind her before she heard anything, but she held her instinctive reaction. She was becoming accustomed to the approach of her scout.

"No need to give me warnings like that little one."

"That was for my own safety. I don't want to surprise a dragon. It's not a safe way to live."

Roark smiled at the relaxed manner that they were talking to each other. She felt a sudden relaxation settle over her.

"Have we actually survived this?" she asked in a quiet whisper, unwilling to say the words too loud. She still believed that witches of the spine listened for things like that.

"It would seem so."

Roark sighed. She was tired, but she could not deny that she was happy with how this had turned out. Elsa was lost, and that was a sad outcome, but she had given her life to protect the princess. Her sacrifice was not in vain.

"Have you met the Princess' suitor?"

"No. I have read his correspondence, but that is all."

Roark looked at the girl for a moment to make sure which smile she was using. It told her all she needed to know. Roark nodded her acceptance of the girls answer.

Together they stood looking across the field into the lands of Parthia. It seemed impossible that they had made it and the pair stood together enjoying the silence of their success. Malich's Guardian's gathered the bodies of the wizard's army in both Arandor and Partihian colors throughout the rest of the day. They all shared a meal on the border awaiting the dawn, and they finally had to gag Cinnia's father before they could rest.

~~~

With the dawn Roark stood again on the border and scanned the edge of the forest that opened into a fallow field. The farmhouse in the distance was just rising to continue to manage the harvest. As was common, they paid little attention to the edge of another world.

Roark looked back at her own retinue for the meeting at the border. Malich stood ready with their banner. Cinnia and her ladies were standing ready. Even the wizard King stood trussed, gagged, and smoldering with anger at being treated so poorly. Satisfied they were ready Roark again looked across the field at the sun crested ridge.

Roark sampled the air around her for signs of an ambush. It was safe, for the moment, but she dared not relax until the Princess was safe across the border.

She nodded to Malich. He stepped across the border and beyond the trees. He stopped where he could be seen and braced the pole he carried with his foot. The banner floated from his hand into the light breeze. As soon as the colors were visible, two men who sat on horses on the crest each raised their lances from across their shields and placed them on their braces. Two banners streamed away from them in the wind. Roark recognized both the crest of the Crown Prince and the Lord Marshal of Parthia.

Everyone was cautious. There were too many chances for ambush and double cross in encounters like this. Everyone looked for traps. Distrust was the name of the game in border encounters.

The Parthian knights crossed the field at a canter and watched the edges of the forest for archers or movement. Each man wore full combat plate armor. The lances were covered with the banners. Even though they seemed decorative, Roark had no doubt that beneath them rested sharp and capable points designed to penetrate similar armor and gut anyone not wearing any. Although each man seemed relaxed as they rode across the field, she could feel their scrutiny cut through the brush and foliage. They reached the edge with a separation that gave them space and time to protect their liege and turned with precision to face the way they had come.

An entourage led by a well-dressed young man in light riding armor crested the field and rode up to meet the man at the border.

As they approached, Roark walked out of the woods to make herself and her party apparent. The Princess followed with Reva beside her. Alexa prodded the bound king ahead of her.

"Well met Guardian. I received a message that you were delivering my betrothed this day, here. This is an unusual place to cross the border between our realms."

Roark stepped out of the mass and ahead of her First.

"Yes, it is, intentionally so."

The Crown Prince of Parthia adjusted his facing to her and rolled his shoulders back as if her movements were dangerous.

"You are Roark?" he asked with some alarm.

"I expect surprise. I have never been seen in this form for an exchange. But I am Roark."

The Prince stepped down from his horse and managed the bridle himself. He was a young man, but that was what Roark had expected. It took youth to be open to new ideas.

The Prince then surprised everyone. He bowed to the Guardian. It was a sign of respect rarely shown to anyone who was not of equal or higher rank.

Roark returned the bow and waited.

"You deserve my respect. I have been looking into some events that came to my attention. As I am the Lord Marshal of Parthia as well as the Crown Prince I have specific interest in what happens at our borders. You have taken a great risk for me specifically and my realm generally."

Roark remained silent. There was nothing to be gained by making more of what everyone knew.

"You have brought my love through danger to safety at high cost to yourself. At the least, you have my appreciation and respect. If you will have it, you have my promise of support and the support of the Lord Marshal of Parthia."

Roark bowed again in a sign that she accepted his offer but said nothing more.

The Princess stepped forward and bowed to her betrothed. He offered his hand and she placed her's in his palm. He smiled at her and drew her to his side.

"Wilhelm, my two ladies will travel with me and I would like to offer a place in Parthia to Roark. She has proven a very capable escort and would certainly benefit your kingdom," Cinna said as she stepped up to take her place with him.

"I can deny you nothing my love, and anyone who has done what Roark has done for me and you is welcome in Parthia."

Roark bowed again to the Prince in a show of respect and then looked back over her shoulder toward the Spine and her prisoner.

"My place is in the Spine. I am the Guardian of those passes and as long as men like these feel justified to do what they please in them, I will need to keep watch."

She motioned to Malich to bring Garth, the wizard and King of Arandor forward.

Prince Wilhelm noted the man Malich brought forward and immediately recognized him. He immediately bowed to the bound man. The Prince was faced with a problem that Roark knew would be difficult, but it was the responsibility of the Lord Marshal to deal with all accusations such as this. It was inappropriate for the King of Arandor to be bound, but Roark required it for their safety.

Wilhelm looked at her and patiently waited for an explanation, and it was clear an explanation was required.

"I turn this prisoner over to the King of Parthia through his Lord Marshal. You may do with him what you please, but for his crimes he is permanently banned from passing through or entering The Dragon's Spine."

"By whose authority do you make this decree?" Wilhelm asked. "There is no recognized government within that realm. It is a free realm which any can pass."

"That is not true. You know it is not and even if it was, conditions have changed," Roark answered with an arrogance that surprised both men who now stood together looking at Roark. Cinna watched at the arm of the Parthian Prince and away from her father.

"How exactly has it changed? I have an interest in how that realm is managed as it borders Parthia."

"Yes, it does. It borders Arandor as well. Since I have both of you, I will make this announcement once."

Roark raised both of her arms to her side as if she could encompass the entirety of the Spine with them and looked directly at each man.

"All of the realms that touch the Dragon's Spine have acted as if it was their trash heap. You have sent your troops across her borders."

Both men started to make a comment and she held up her hand. She pointed to the bodies being brought forward by her Guardians. Each dressed in the attire of both realms.

"You accosted those who were within those borders. You trapped those who you deemed unacceptable between your borders."

She dropped her arms and stepped toward both men.

"No longer will you send your outcasts into the Spine."

She pointed directly at the wizard.

"No longer will you send your troops across her borders."

She looked at Wilhelm.

"I have few complaints with your realm, but you have some within your kingdom that charge usurious rates to allow people to cross your border. This must stop and be better managed. I will no longer allow the inhabitants of The Dragon's Spine to be treated this way by any realm."

"You have no authority..." The wizard King spat his first response and Roark silenced him with her dagger pointing at his larynx.

"I am the authority of this realm now. I have the right to take your life. I caught you in my realm with an invading force. You have left a trail of bodies along a path from the border with your realm all the way to this border with Parthia. I am being lenient by not killing you here, but you know why that is. Do you wish to challenge my claim?"

He said nothing more and simply shook his head.

"I have granted your daughter's request. You have one year. After that, I will come for you, and what I do to your realm will depend entirely on what you do in the next months."

"What right do you have to take this authority?" Wilhelm asked in a calm and arbitrating tone.

"It is called The Dragon's Spine because it has been ruled by a family of dragons. I am the only surviving member of that family. I cannot prove currently that the death of my adoptive family was an attempt to kill me, but I am the last of my kind that I know of. I am the rightful ruler of this realm. Those who wish to challenge me can do so, legally. Send your grievances to me and I will answer them directly."

Wilhelm nodded his approval of her statement. He recognized her right.

"I challenge your authority to take this position." Garth roared, finding his courage and a legal way that would not involve a physical encounter.

Wilhelm raised his hand as the protest was lodged.

"As Lord Marshal of Parthia, and a neutral party with authority in these matters, I will hear the protest. At this time, I recognize her authority. I know the laws of these realms and the history of the rulers of The Dragon's Spine. In a month we will meet at my court to discuss these matters."

Garth shook his head. "I would prefer a stay for that hearing. I require a chance to get back to Arandor. I need my aides and information I have there regarding the lawful abdication of authority. It will take me that long to get back. Release me now so that I may get there and back to challenge these claims."

Wilhelm shook his head. "You should send for what you need and stay in Parthia until I can hear the claim."

Garth's face turned pale. He knew the situation he was in and understood the power the Lord Marshal had. He was asking. Garth said nothing, but his opinion was clear.

"I also recognize her right, as a representative of the ruling family, to ban your travel through her realm. You may travel to Arandor if you so wish, but you must take either the Northern Steppes or the Southern Ocean to do so."

"I can never make that in the time you set."

"That may be so, but I am not changing my time to hear her evidence. It is her right to have her claims decided in a timely period. All evidence will be in my court in thirty days or it will be considered void after that. It is up to you to do what you need to answer her claims in that time."

Roark looked calmly at Garth. He was boiling with anger that she had been able to trap him so. It was an obvious ploy since she knew he could still travel magically. Perhaps the wizard King didn't want it known throughout the realms that he was a wizard. She smiled at him as she found yet another tool to use against him, then turned her attention to the last pieces of her plan.

"Lord Marshal, I will leave him to you to deal with, but I have charges that he has repeatedly injured and assaulted the people of The Dragon's Spine. If he returns to my borders, I will have him arrested to face charges for all of his deeds within my realm."

Wilhelm nodded his acceptance of her decree.

"I appreciate your offer and hope that I may visit the Princess occasionally."

"You are welcome in Parthia at any time. Please visit when you are able." The Lord Marshal reached into his blouse and removed an amulet from his neck. He then bowed to her again and passed it to her.

"This will guarantee your passage through my realm. My father would enjoy meeting you. I believe he knew your father."

Roark could not help but smile at the statement. She did not know anything of her actual parents. She only knew of her adopted family that she had been sent to for protection.

"Perhaps when I am there for the hearing."

"I will make sure he is ready to receive you."

Roark bowed to the Prince one final time and he turned to his horse and the aide of his future bride.

Roark looked at Reva who stood behind her Lady. She put out her hand to the young scout and she took it.

"I have a need for someone with your talents if you are available and can secure the permission of your Lady."

Reva grinned her mischievous smile and then looked back at the Princess. Cinnia, who had been focused on leaving, paused for a moment then gave a nearly imperceptible nod. Reva stepped away from her and toward Roark.

They embraced on the border of the two lands where the beginning of a long-lasting agreement was forged. Then turned together and ran side-by-side into the trees. Neither Malich nor the others could see them as they vanished into the cover of The Dragon's Spine.

NOTE FROM THE AUTHOR

Thank you for reading this Action-Adventure Fantasy set in the world of the Dragon's Spine. If you have enjoyed this adventure, please consider leaving me a review on the retail site where you purchased or downloaded this novel.

I know I enjoyed creating this world and all the events in this story. I am continuing to create more stories about Roark and the Guardians. I hope you keep an eye out for those as they are being created. You can check in with me on my blog for more information and even new stories.

If you are interested in other stories and novels I have available, please find them at all online retailers in e-book and paperback formats.

Follow me on Facebook:
https://www.facebook.com/tdraufson

OTHER BOOKS BY T.D. RAUFSON

Legacy of Dragons Series:
Legacy of Dragons: Emergence
Legacy of Dragons: Resurgence

The Queen's Yeoman